LUCID DREAMS

By

Josephene Stull

Josephene Stull ©2013
Published by Thoroughbred Press LLC
ISBN-10: 0991408217
ISBN-13: 978-0-9914082-1-4

About the author

Josephene Stull has always loved to write. However, life took a number of twists and turns before she actually committed to pursuing her dream of becoming a published author. Her dream came true when her first novel, co-authored with Carolyn Owens, titled *Witches, Bitches, and Good Ol' Boys*, was published by Solstice Publishing in 2012.

Books by Josephene Stull

Witches, Bitches, and Good ol' Boys
(co-authored with Carolyn Owens)

Website:
www.TheGreasedQuill.com

Acknowledgments

I would like to acknowledge Lucas Xavier Stull for his excellent work designing the cover for Lucid Dreams.

I would also like to thank Stefan Vucak for a superb editing job. I found him knowledgeable, easy to work with and highly professional.

Lucid Dreams

CHAPTER ONE

The smell of perspiration, stale cigar smoke, and something else Angel McKeough's sleep induced brain processed as rancid semen stung her nostrils, although logically, semen would not have such a vile discernible odor. She willed her body to remain still while her eyes adjusted to the semi-darkness. Her heart thumped wildly. *Some pervert must have followed her home from work.* She rotated her eyes, expecting to glimpse a dark figure lurking in a corner, but there was nobody.

She flicked on the bedside lamp and sat upright, hugging a pillow against her chest. Her pupils grew round. She was completely naked, except for a fishnet pantyhose hanging precariously half on, half off, her left foot.

Her hair clung to her face and bare breasts. She raked the sweat-drenched strands of hair aside. The scream rising in her throat changed to a self-conscious giggle. The malodor was emanating from her. Her long locks had soaked up the pungent stench of *Club Venus* like a sponge. Thanks to her sweatbox apartment, her scalp had an extremely unpleasant odor.

"Ugh!"

After a double shift at the titty bar, she must have been so exhausted, she'd stripped down and passed out on the bed. Angel shook her head. She vaguely remembered dumping Alex, her three-year-old son, onto his bed and twisting the shower knobs full on.

The sound of running water sent her sprinting to the bathroom *au naturel.* She twisted the shower knobs

1

backward and stood stock still in the middle of the floor staring at water droplets hanging from the ceiling. The shower had run full blast all night.

"Damn!"

More overtime hours at the club.

She reached for a hairbrush and began to stroke her tangles into long, velvet black strands that framed her face.

She once again turned the water on and stepped underneath the showerhead, gasping as icy water washed over her body. She lathered quickly; then stepped out and toweled vigorously until her skin glowed a tantalizing pink and her nipples were vivid rubies.

Loosely pinning her hair on the back of her head, she rummaged through the small hole in the bedroom wall that served as a closet. She chose a well-worn pair of blue jeans and a Disney tweety bird T-shirt Alex liked. She moved to the chest of drawers and took out a pair of white cotton briefs.

"Peachy! About as exciting as a dirty sock," she muttered, pushing the drawer shut.

A sudden surge of recklessness hit her. She pulled the drawer open a crack and stuffed back the plain briefs. Her fingers hovered near the top drawer. Biting her lip, she slid the drawer wide and removed a six by eight black lacquered box inlaid with tiny mother of pearl roses. She closed her eyes, tracing the outline of each tiny delicate flower with her fingertips. She sucked in a gulp of air and exhaled slowly before lifting the lid to disclose a pair of black lace panties and matching brassiere neatly folded on a lining of white satin.

Tears spilled over and ran down her cheeks as she

stared at her wedding attire. Charlie had called her a naughty girl for wearing black underneath the beautiful white wedding gown, but it didn't stop him from stripping those same panties from her body with his teeth. She smiled slightly and rubbed the flimsy scraps of lace against her cheek, remembering.

Angel wiggled into the low-cut panties, adjusted them over her crotch and fumbled with the brassiere. Her trembling fingers struggled to connect the hook as she attempted to fit her D-size breasts into C-size cups.

Suddenly, she froze. The hair on the back of her neck started to rise and a lump lodged in her throat. She had an overwhelming sensation that someone was watching her.

She picked the family bible off the bedside table and moved cautiously from room to room, but found nothing. Weird things had been happening much too often lately and the tempo was picking up.

"Stress. It's got to be stress," she muttered.

Looking at bare breasts, g-stringed butts and horny peckers for up to ten hours a night was affecting her badly. Not the blatant slap and tickle action in itself; she was finished with men and that type foolishness. Their lewd conduct was vile and disgusting.

The sense of an invisible eye watching her was psyching her out. Her search of the rooms had turned up empty, just as it had numerous times before. She shrugged. Sleep deprivation was kicking her imagination into overdrive. She breathed a sigh of relief and giggled at her choice of weapon. The bible was big and heavy. In the event she encountered something unholy, not that she believed in ghosts and demons, she would have the means to banish them, and if the perpetrator was human, she had the ability to knock the Peeping Tom on his backside.

"You gotta stop that, girl," she said, frowning when she realized she was talking to herself again.

She wanted Charlie back. At the thought, her face darkened. Charlie had promised he'd always love her and never leave her, but he lied. All men were liars!

She fingered the revealing strips of her lacy bra, cupping the voluptuous breasts in her hands. Without Charlie's touch, these excessive mounds of flesh just weighed her down. Her hands slid across her abdomen, glided over the scanty lace panties and around the contours of her well rounded buttocks. She liked the feel of satin and lace against her skin. These undergarments had been reserved for Charlie's eyes only, but he would not be coming back. He had put on his little golden halo, spread his angel wings and flown away, leaving her to carry on without him.

She laughed bitterly. He had been her pillar of strength and an anchor when storm clouds gathered in her perfect little world. Leaving, he left her lonely, vulnerable, and afraid of her own shadow...and an imaginary stalker.

She screamed shrilly as the strap snapped on her brassiere and one breast burst free. After her heart had settled, she found the situation immensely funny.

"Hey! Invisible presence, get a load of this." She giggled.

She slipped on jeans and T-shirt. The tingling sensation of goose pimples made her wish she'd held her tongue.

CHAPTER TWO

All festivities ground to a halt the moment Garmin Maximilian stepped through the entrance to the great hall of Hel's Castle. The voices dwindled to an occasional whisper spoken into cupped palms. When the Number One Hellhound, a title conferred by the Mistress of Hell because of his extraordinary *abilities* and demon ancestry, honored a social gathering with his presence, he was usually on the hunt for runaway dishonored dead that were attempting to escape the endless torment of the lowest level of hell for a more desirable realm of the underworld.

All eyes turned in his direction, and lips stretched into practiced smiles, but he did not acknowledge a single presence with as much as a nod.

His gaze swept the room. He didn't give a rat's ass about the assemblage of servile court sycophants, and he didn't have any intention of engaging in conversation with these double-tongued dregs of society.

He gestured with his hands and, on cue, the festivities resumed. He kept to the shadows, out of sight of the probing gaze of social wallflowers whose timid smiles didn't quite mask the frustration and natural urge to merge reflected in their china doll faces.

The air reeked of musty armpits, yeasty loins, and the pungent fusion of dozens of aromatic fragrances intended to mask these malodorous discharges.

Court jesters jingled their bells and frolicked around him, and musicians twanged their instruments loudly, but he didn't hear them.

Painted ladies circled the ballroom in their lace and velvet gowns and cast amorous glances over the shoulders of their dance partners at the solitary figure, but Garmin turned a blind eye to their suggestive behavior.

The heels of his boots echoed eerily on the cold marble tiles as he shouldered his way through the crowd, moving to stand by a window scarcely larger than an arrow slit. His knuckles whitened as he gripped the stone ledge and stared out at the well-traveled bridge a stone's throw from the main gate. The bridge served solely as a one-way passage for the dead to enter the realm of the underworld where they were destined to remain for all eternity. It had remained an impregnable fortification for thousands of years, but he was not daunted by the architectural ingenuity of the ancients.

Today was the day of reckoning. A cold chill ran along the length of his spine as Garmin stared at the formidable dank cloud hovering above the ancient castle. Even inside the stone walls, he could hear the river clamoring incessantly under hand hewn logs that gave rise to massive wooden timbers.

Turbulent waves slapped against the bridge with hurricane force as the water continuously churned against a sea of bones long since gnawed clean by the largest serpent ever to draw breath and its smaller kin.

His face clouded. If his mission failed, his lot would be cast. He, too, would be left to the mercy of the gigantic, venom spitting sea serpent lurking in the river's depths, and the mighty serpent knew no mercy.

The hollow sound of bone grating against bone made him question his timeless existence. He was certain he had not been born in the misty abode of the dead, but this place had literally laid claim to his state of being as it had those souls who had been cast down into this hellish existence.

Part man, part beast, he was unlike any other in the vast realms of the Kingdom of the Dead. He had no beginning and no end. He just was…the last seed of his kind. The only thing he could justifiably attest to his existence was his name. It was an honorable name carried forward from his father. Garmin, meaning spearman, had a ring of victory, and Maximilian proclaimed greatness.

His chest swelled. For a fleeting second, his normally expressionless face was etched with a faint smile. He shifted his gaze to a faded picture in a magnificent gold frame hanging above the mantel. A proud warrior stared out from the ornate circle of glass; his shaggy lineaments highlighted by disproportionately narrow, close-set eyes, glacier blue and twice as cold. His father, he'd been told.

The man's uniform, bedecked with medals of honor, stretched tightly across a massive chest. On the breast pocket, the name Maximilian was displayed in bold black letters. Yet, his image hung upside down to signify he had lost favor with the one known as The Dark Mother.

"Mother!"

A humorless chuckle followed his exclamation. The term *mother* was loosely applied. The Dark Mother did not project the slightest semblance of a maternal being. She was mistress of the underworld and its inhabitants, and exercised such despotic abuse of dominance over her subjects that even a mutinous thought could bring repercussions of unspeakable horrors.

He studied the face of his father, marveling at its

grizzly-like magnificence. He was disappointed to note he bore little resemblance to his sire. His distinguishing characteristics and dung colored eyes could have come from none other than his birth mother, a cruel twist of fate since he knew nothing of the human bitch that pushed him out of her belly.

His earliest memories revolved around The Dark Mother. He'd been kept close to the hip of this supreme being as if he was shackled to her tit. Inquisitive questions regarding his *real* mother were met with extreme hostility. And when *Mother* was displeased, even the ironwood forest trembled. He had stopped asking questions and excluded all thoughts of his birth mother from his consciousness.

He snorted sarcastically. In spite of his dominant human genes, his resemblance to his earthly mother was only superficial. Caged inside his puny six foot-six physique was a dominant primordial beast cast from the same mold as his eminent sire, with a taste for warm flesh and a thirst for fresh blood.

He would have liked to adopt this primal personality as his primary identity, but his instincts told him to do so would give the beast inside him too much power and, eventually, it would absorb his alternate self. He had been born a splitling and had no desire to assimilate into a singular being. He'd learned to subdue the beast and to bring it forth on command.

That had not always been the case. His eyes glazed as he traveled back in time. The Dark Mother had preyed on his innocence. She'd molded and shaped him to suit her callused projection of the ultimate male, patterned after her. A mere child, he'd carried out her sadistic prime directives with such precision, grown men trembled in his wake, but those first transformations ground on his nerves.

His affliction had become his addiction. He wanted more…endless possibilities. He'd toyed with the phenomena of shapeshifting until he'd not only mastered the art, but taken it to a higher level. Soon, he would put his skills to the ultimate test. He laughed, a dry monotonous sound devoid of mirth or feeling. It could hardly be considered a challenge, since he had an ace up his sleeve. However, he hadn't been chosen to stand at the side of The Dark Mother as her Number One by making nice and playing fair.

His lips thinned. In spite of the pomp and circumstance afforded the coveted title, he'd known the first time he dared to climb onto the high seat, where The Dark Mother sat in judgment of the dead, and gazed into the crystal skull crowning the royal scepter that his destiny lay along the same path blazed by his father.

Through his personal looking glass, he could see the world of the living, a cesspool of pussy from the looks of brazen hussies openly displaying their wares, but he had eyes for only one woman. From the moment he first set eyes on her, he was caught like a catfish on a hook. A lustful seed sprouted inside his loins. His concupiscence for the raven haired beauty infiltrated his brain to such an extent, a fleeting thought of her birddogged his pecker to stand on point. He wanted to thrust his shaft all the way inside her belly, not ogle her through a crystal peephole like a lovesick adolescent who had yet to get his dick wet.

He was going to find his crystal princess and bring

her home, a decision that would undoubtedly result in a series of unpleasant eventualities.

He squared his shoulders. It was done. He had made up his mind and he wasn't backing down. The journey, an uncharted course, would not be easy. He would be guided only by bits of information he'd managed to patch together, some primal itch that could only be scratched by the capable hands of his preferred mate, and a small still voice inside his head that whispered, 'Go!'

One hurdle stood in his way—the keeper of the bridge or, The Maiden, as she preferred to be called.

The old soul warden had guarded the bridge for hundreds, maybe thousands of years. He suspected that even she had long since lost count of her years of service. Her prowess in battle was legendary. Many unhappy dead had challenged her command, but not one solitary soul had returned back across the bridge once the gates of hell had swung shut behind them.

A roguish grin whitewashed his face. In spite of her impeccable record, the old biddy was about to get her feathers plucked, and she wouldn't even know she'd been defeathered until it was too late.

He glanced at the benches lining the walls of the great hall, pleased to note most were vacant. "Good!" He stood an excellent chance of taking his leave unseen.

Odeen came. He had been flowing faster than ever he had flowed before.

He sensed eyes watching him and turned quickly before The Dark Mother could avert her gaze. He flashed a knowing look in her direction and boldly matched her stare, amused to see a spark of interest flicker in the icy depths of her eyes before she shielded them from view underneath her cowl.

He was playing with fire, but he'd be long gone before The Dark Mother made up her mind whether she wished to punish him for his insolence or ravish him. This was not the first time he had caught her giving him the once-over. He hoped she was not fostering a desire to whore with him as, accordingly to legend, she had sought to do with his father. He had no intention of allowing his minion as her Number One to evolve to anything close to that level of intimacy. *Hell no!*
Garmin Maximilian would rather crush his balls between two boulders and let the last seed of his ancestral line soak into the dust than grind his meat between those emaciated pubic bones.

He disappeared into the crowd and exited the great hall. He glanced toward the lone figure on the bridge standing steadfast at her post. He lifted his hand in a mock salute and stepped forward to pit his ingenuity against The Maiden's wile, wit, wisdom, and sword-wielding wizardry.

"Showtime," he mumbled. "Break a leg, bitch!"

CHAPTER THREE

The Maiden noted with a start that the massive iron gates were opening, a highly unusual occurrence since no word had come from The Dark Mother's chambers that company was coming. A stickler for routine, she tapped her foot impatiently and waited to herd the latest journey of souls into the afterlife.

To her surprise, the gates suddenly slammed shut, followed by the distinctive click of a key turning inside the massive locks. She whipped around with her nose up. Her senses detected nothing, but her instincts told her something was amiss.

Too late, she realized her mistake in thinking the gates had opened to allow someone to enter. Someone or something had gotten out and passed her by! The warm breeze, which caressed her weather-beaten face for the briefest moment had not come from the weather. The bastard creature, whether it walked on two legs or four, had mockingly blown its hot breath on her cheek in a whisper of a kiss.

She inhaled deeply. A vaporous cloud seeded with aromatic fragrances of lilac, jasmine, spices and dung made it virtually impossible to hone in on a scent trail. How was she going to apprehend the culprit when the whole damn place smelled like someone has taken a shit in the flower garden?

Her fingers balled into fists. The son-of-a-bitch was fucking with her. He was rubbing her nose in it and laughing behind her back, and she was powerless to stop him.

Her burst of anger tapered off quickly. The Maiden wrung her hands in agitation. The Dark Mother would not be pleased. The punishment for her carelessness would be quick coming and of long duration.

She threw back her head and opened her mouth. A scream powered by a jolt of raw adrenaline soared upward, punching through the vast nothingness. Her anguished cry slowly petered out to a mere whimper of a wounded animal. She spread her arms and began to chant.

Keepers of this timeless place
Show to me the unseen face of
The one who dared to hide and tread
Across this bridge of those long dead.

Hooded figures appeared out of the mist. Faceless silhouettes with folded arms silently watched her and waited for her to speak.

She pleaded her case, ranting and raving about some invisible being, but the gathering of keepers had no answers and dismissed her plight as unsubstantiated ramblings. They dissipated back into the mist without a word of advice or backward glance.

"Useless!" she screamed after them, but the barrier of silence was broken only by the sound of her own voice.

The whole damn bunch had looked at her as if she was stark raving mad. She crossed her arms across her chest. Let them look. Her secret was locked safely inside the cavities of her cranial vault. Only she knew this world had taken her identity and erased memories of her past.

"What's in a name?" she muttered.

The Maiden had served her well as a title. Whoever

she might have been in a past life no longer existed. She knew everything worth remembering.

Liar! A voice screamed inside her head. There was more; something most precious had been lost...gone and forgotten.

She shook her head. She knew what she knew. Someone had gone missing, although she could offer no plausible explanation as to how he'd managed to slip pass. She lifted her shoulders and let them drop as if a horrendous weight pulled them down. The thought of a face-to-face confrontation with The Dark Mother struck terror into her heart. But whatever happened, she would not whimper and grovel for mercy. Her bones rattled as she stretched her five-foot frame to the maximum. She blew a few straggly strands of hair off her face and drew her tattered rags around her body in a futile effort to ward off the numbing cold of a wayward wind blowing across the river.

"What price eternity?" she whispered.

She gazed longingly through the small window of the great hall, and her eyes fixed on the flickering orange glow. Fire demons climbed the sides of a fallen timber and danced merrily inside the stone fireplace, spewing sparks of glowing embers across the floor.

The inhabitants of that place ate, drank, and danced, while famine was her knife, hunger her fork, starvation her table, and misery her bed.

"To hell with 'em," she screamed into the wind, "To hell with 'em all!"

She turned and stared at a group of stark ancient relics dotting the landscape. Shrouded by a low hanging mist, seemingly rising from the bowels of the earth, the moss covered stones leaned haphazardly against one another. An unconscious sigh passed her lips. Those resting there were the lucky ones.

She plucked a broken sword from the river. She would run the blunt-ended weapon through the elusive blackguard who went past her and pin him to the bridge, while she peeled off long, thin, fleshy ribbons of skin to tie around the bastard's balls when she presented them to The Dark Mother as atonement for her dereliction of duty.

But before the spirit waned, she'd gouge out his eyes with her fingernails. Her face would be the last thing he took with him to the hall of the damned.

She began to hum and chant in a language strange even to her own ears. A form slowly took shape from the mist rising off the water.

"Aaaah! It's you is it?"

A wave of disappointment washed over her. This fish was too big for her pond. She'd have to take second chair in deciding the fate of The Dark Mother's Number One. She snorted. "Number one asshole."

She speculated on his actions. What compelling force could have prompted him to run the risk of bringing down The Dark Mother's wrath on himself?

A plan began to form in The Maiden's mind. Her face split into a malicious grin. As a general rule, this sordid character would be untouchable, but Sir Garmin had opened the gateway of opportunity. For years, she'd watched him stroll boldly about the castle grounds, so full of himself even The Dark Mother was deceived by his grandiosity, and dreamed of having him in her grip.

His Highness would be back. Due to his stature with

The Dark Mother, she'd have to let him back across the bridge eventually, but she'd delay his entry as long as possible, allowing The Dark Mother's hostility to ripen, deflecting more rage toward the prodigal Number One and less toward the keeper of the bridge.

She shuddered at the thought of facing The Dark Mother and owning her transgression of letting the sneaky bastard slip past her watch. However, in spite of the fact The Dark Mother had a zero tolerance for failure, once she explained the extenuating circumstances, she was confident The Dark Mother would not be inclined to cut off her foot to punish her toe.

The Maiden emptied her lungs with a stupendous whoosh of air. She almost felt a tiny spark of remorse for the fate of the high and mighty Garmin Maximilian. Almost!

CHAPTER FOUR

A slight breeze ruffled Garmin's wolf pelt loincloth as he stood in the pale glow of a waning moon and waited, questioning his sanity. He had dared much and risked all, and he was completely ignorant as to the rationale behind such a foolhardy venture. He understood all too well the urge to copulate. Everything had needs, even the beasts of the fields and streams. But it was more; something deeper and more compelling had forced him to climb astride his stallion, Midnight, and make this incredible journey into the unknown, in search of a woman he had only viewed remotely, when he could have taken any bitch in the kingdom to his bed. He chuckled dryly. As a matter of fact, he had already done that very thing more times than he could openly admit without appearing to be a braggart. Those adulteress whores meant nothing to him. If his intended mate ever dared to cuckold him, he'd take out his peg and stitching awl and sew her slit together so tightly, she'd bloat and pop like a ripe carcass.

As the last link in the evolutionary chain of Kanimorphs, he wanted to preserve the species in his image, not begat a whole new strain of mutants alien to his race. As a means to an end, he'd set his sights on a bride from the earthly plane. He didn't give a duck fuck if his picture *did* end ass up above the stone hearth alongside that of his father.

There wasn't even a flicker of warmth in the rich amber depths of his eyes as he followed the movements of the woman stepping out of the Yellow Stripe Cab, but his loins were a wildfire burning out of control.

He watched as she hopped on one foot to adjust the strap on her high heel shoe before moving up the walkway. Chilly bumps popped on his body. The rhythmic dance of the woman's hips pleased him as she zigzagged around deep cracks in the sidewalk leading toward the dreary apartment building in a shady district of East New York City. His heart raced as lustful urges hammered his manhood. He lifted his head, flaring his nostrils to soak up the woman's tantalizing scent. His lips pulled back, revealing brilliant white teeth that sharply contrasted the cinnamon flesh bronzed by the sands of time, but showing no sign of weathering.

He'd been watching the woman for two days and had not been disappointed at what he'd seen. He *was* troubled by the fact she always seemed to have a mini human parasite hanging off her hip.

He slid from the shadows and watched her struggle under the weight of the sleeping child as she climbed the steep stairs. He liked the way her skirt clung to the contours of her ungirdled hindquarters. He had a thing for callipygian women, and this one was exemplary. The sight of her two humps sliding past each other underneath her garment ignited a passion that threatened to unravel his carefully laid plans.

The hinge squeaked and groaned as he jumped and grasped a ladder dangling from a horizontal platform attached to the wall of the building. He climbed the steps and squatted on the steel grating outside the woman's window. He could hear the door slam and the woman's husky voice calling out, "Alex!"

So the fungus had a name! He watched as she threw her

house keys on the coffee table, grunting his displeasure as she disappeared from sight with the boy across her shoulder.

When she came back, he gasped in admiration as she shook loose the restraints that bound her long flowing mane. He was awed by the way the flickering neon signs and billboards changed her silky ebony strands to a hazy shade of purple. He waited in anticipation as she plucked the large hoop rings from her ears, plopped them down beside her keys and undid the top buttons on her silk blouse. A soft sigh escaped his lips.

Any other man might have felt a twinge of guilt at the ecstasy in his loins as he watched from his coveted position, but he wasn't any other man. He was Garmin Maximilian. He did exactly as he pleased, and no one dared try and stop him.

He waited with bated breath as the woman removed her blouse and carefully laid it over the back of a faux leather chair, plucking at the folds. She then undid the zipper on her skirt, wiggling her hips to allow it and the undergarment to slide past her curves and glide down her thighs, caressing the creamy white skin.

His eyes traveled down her shapely legs and back to the subtle bulge in the crotch. He started to pant, making small animal sounds as his member hardened. He wanted to take her there and then, but the timing wasn't right. The first streaks of dawn would soon infiltrate the shadows where he crouched. It appeared he had erred in thinking he would draw less attention to himself by shedding his royal fashions for the simpler basic loincloth. Every time he stepped out of the shadows, all hell broke loose. He must be away before prying eyes sought him out.

He quickly descended to the street. He threw back his head and moaned, the sound amplified into a loud, frustrated cry of unfulfilled longing. He pressed himself deeper into the shadows as the woman threw open the window.

"Damn!"

His jaw dropped. She had discarded her brassiere. Brazenly exposed pale mounds of creamy flesh shadowed her small waist. He was unable to take his eyes off the swollen bounty. He begin to hump, thrusting his manhood forward, air fucking.

He grasped his member, pushing it downward in a titanic effort to constrain his feral instincts. He could wait. The wait would make the coupling all the sweeter. He doubted if such a fragile creature could survive the union, but the prospect was too intriguing to abort the mission.

Time was on his side...nine days coming, nine days to take care of business, and nine days to return. The Dark Mother had been generous indeed, although he knew perfectly well she didn't have the slightest inkling that he would follow through with his request, much less be successful in his endeavor to get past The Maiden.

****

Garmin was weary from his travels and suddenly realized he had taken neither food nor drink since his arrival from the underworld two days past. The coils of his intestines squeezed against one another so fiercely he feared they were consuming each other.

Lucid Dreams

The emptiness in his belly incensed the beast in him. The gluttonous cravings demanded more than a quick meal. The primal instinct to hunt overshadowed his libidinous desires.

Human figures had scuttled around like cockroaches during the hours of light, but had disappeared when the shadows claimed the streets.

For a brief moment, he worried that he might have to blow his cover and snatch a hearty specimen from the jaws of the vehicles rolling along the city streets at excessive speeds. But in a few moments, his keen ears detected faltering footsteps. His eyes pierced the darkness and locked on a lone figure stumbling up the street, clutching a bottle-shaped brown paper bag.

Garmin drew deeper into the shadows and crouched low. His lips curled with contempt at the vile odor of vomit and whiskey clinging to the man, but with dawn streaking the sky red, he had to act fast.

His hand shot out and encased the man's head, pulling the struggling figure against his naked body. He grasped the tattered T-shirt, jerked it past the man's head, then lifted him by his throat and shook him until the trousers and grimy footgear slipped free. With one fluid motion, he peeled the dingy briefs from the man's body and tossed them aside. His lips drew back in a snarl as the man tightened his flanks and tried to conceal his danglers between crossed legs. *This pitiful piece of trash thought he was going to be violated! Hardly!*

Garmin Maximilian would rather ram his rod down the throat of a swamp beast than up the ass of this street vermin.

He cuffed the man's mouth with his palm, stifling

21

the man's screams. His teeth tore through soft flesh, latched onto the man's neck and he suckled the jugular. The warm, salty, crimson flow quenched his ravenous thirst, and the soft, greasy flesh filled the hollow spot in his gut, but the ingestion of the heart left him feeling giddy instead of empowering him with strength and vigor.

He licked the blood from his body and picked up the scattered meager strips of cloth. He slipped the trousers and raggedy shirt over his muscular frame, but left the undergarment where it had fallen. Local protocol required he cover himself, but he was not going to truss his manhood inside that cock strangler. His genitals had hung low and free for hundreds of years and they would remain so for hundreds more.

He slid his feet into the grungy shoes, wincing as his toes strained in the small space as he'd once strained against the heavy collar that bound him to The Dark Mother. He rubbed his throat. The leather strip around his neck no longer shackled him. The collar and heavy gold chain were only symbolic tokens of his sworn allegiance to The Dark Mother.

"If you can get past The Maiden, then by all means go," she'd said, and he'd taken her at her word.

He laughed at his cleverness. He'd used his bag of tricks and gotten past her watchdog without a hitch. His passage had surely shattered The Dark Mother's confidence in the gatekeeper, but he cared naught for the abominable retribution The Maiden's negligence would bring on her.

He wondered how the old crone came by the title, *The Maiden.* That wretched being was the poorest excuse for a maiden he'd ever seen. She had the frame of a bird, the strength of an ox, the cunning of a fox, and the temperament of a rattlesnake. If she survived The Dark Mother's wrath, he would have to confront her head on to gain entry back across the bridge.

The woman he intended taking with him on the return journey would complicate things, but the bitch was hot…much hotter in the flesh than a projection inside a crystal sphere. He was tempted to forego the habitual preliminary courtship and move directly to the 'boning' stage of the relationship, but he wasn't going to let her off that easily. She would have to earn the right to claim the title as his bitch. He wanted to hear her beg, hear her squeal, then maybe, just maybe, he'd do her.

****

Garmin was pushing the boundaries of obscurity that darkness provided, but his hunger had returned with a vengeance. The intense gnawing sensation inside his gut did not stem from the fires of an empty belly, but from the thrill of the hunt.

He became aware of a burly figure headed in his direction, a well-dressed fellow with a black suit and a thin strip of colored cloth knotted around his neck. He let the man pass and fell in behind him, keeping himself in the shadows. He padded silently, grinning fiendishly as he watched the man twirl his umbrella. *The poor fool would not be around to see whether or not it rained.*

His raspy laugh deep down his throat caused the man to stop and spin around, his gaze darting as he searched the darkness, but the shadows gave nothing away.

Garmin kept pace. His heart pounded against his rib-cage as the man looked over his shoulder with bugged eyes and ragged breath in search of his invisible foe.

"Can you see me now?" Garmin whispered loudly enough so the man could hear.

The caustic smell of salt tinged his nostrils as perspiration oozed down the man's face and dripped off his chin. Garmin increased his pace, no longer bothering to stay in the shadows. He toyed with the man. He slowed his pace to afford the man a head start, then sprinted within arm's reach and grabbed onto his coattail. He intentionally allowed the garment to slip through his fingers, feeding off the man's fear. He could hear the man's heart thumping inside his chest, exciting him. However, it was becoming increasingly obvious this adventure was not going to provide any more of a combative challenge than his previous prey. He would have to stage his own grand finale.

He slipped out of sight and took a shortcut to head off the man. Laughter bubbled up and he gurgled with mirth as the man appeared around the corner, clutching his heart and looking relieved to have escaped his pursuer.

Garmin leaped from the shadows and growled fiercely. He watched color drain from the man's face as he realized something bad was imminent.

"Remove your clothing," said Garmin, his voice loud and harsh amid the silence of terror. His lips twitched when the man's hands instinctively moved to cover his genitals and hindquarters. *What was up with these creatures and their obsession with assholes?*

As the man slipped out of his clothes, Garmin's eyes

traveled up and down the naked body, disgusted at the mass of blubber. He pointed at the man's shoes. "Give."

When the man squatted to remove the footwear, Garmin noted that fear had shriveled the poor bastard's balls to the size of acorns. He shook his head.

"Pitiful."

He towered over the figure kneeling before him, watching the man's lips move in a silent plea. He extended his hand toward the man and lifted him to his feet, then stepped back, smiled mockingly, and unfolded his canines. He saw the man's eyes go black, his muscles tighten and his face excrete raw terror.

"Who...what *are* you?" the man mumbled. Spittle blubbered out the side of his mouth.

Garmin could hear the piercing screams bubbling up inside the man. He sprang upon him, ignoring the feeble attempts to fight him off with a silly umbrella. The screams were reduced to a faint gurgle as saber cuspids found the jugular and ripped it from the man's throat.

Garmin allowed the blood to flow freely, having no desire to drink or feast upon the carcass. He ripped the head off the limp body and held it aloft, howling in victory. The frightful sound reverberated down the street and trailed off into an eerie pitch.

He cast off his blood-spattered clothing, indulging in a refreshing tongue bath before donning the man's more fashionable attire. He grunted with satisfaction as his feet slipped easily into the soft leather shoes.

He breathed deeply, savoring the sweet smell of a fresh kill again. The wind had changed directions and pushed at his back. Thunder rumbled in the distance and jagged lighting sizzled in the morning sky. Garmin lifted his nose and sniffed the air. A storm was approaching. The morning kept getting better.

He turned toward the woman's apartment block and walked jauntily down the street, his step light and his spirits soaring. He never once looked back at the aftermath of the savage passion that had ravaged his senses.

He sighed happily as the faint sounds of a woman's screams tore the air, and flashing lights from a swarm of black and white vehicles, with their noisemakers going full blast, rushed past to converge on the crime scene.

He smiled. Chaos, death and destruction; a perfect ending to a perfect night.

CHAPTER FIVE

Angel was transported from a fantasy dream state to harsh reality as wailing sirens startled her awake. She leaped out of bed. Force of habit sent her running to check on Alex. She found him curled into a ball, clutching the bed covers around his chin, whimpering. She gathered him in her arms and rained kisses down his tear-stained cheeks.

"It's okay, darling. Go back to sleep. Mommy's right here."

"No" he whispered, pulling the covers over his head. "The man is watching me."

Her gaze instinctively darted around the room. "What man?"

Alex's arm poked from underneath the covers and he pointed at the darkest corner of the room.

"The man is watching you now. I don't like the man, Mommy. Make him go away."

The hair rose on the back of her neck and a chill passed through her body. She could see there was no man in the room, but the air seemed different, charged somehow.

She lifted her hand and slapped the air as the drone of a fly assaulted her ears. *Filthy bloodsuckers!* She hated flies almost as much as she hated this tiny apartment. It was so small it was next to impossible to turn around without bumping against a wall. This was no way to bring up a child, but at the moment, it was the best she could manage.

She turned back to Alex.

"Would you like to sleep in Mommy's bed, swee-theart? It's much too early to be up and about on a Saturday morning. You'll have forgotten all about the nasty old man when you wake."

"He's gone now," said Alex. He snuggled down and drifted back to sleep.

Angel rubbed her arms, surprised to find her flesh pimpled. She was no stranger to the sound of sirens. Something was always going down in the neighborhood. Judging from the noise, there must be a dozen squad cars nearby. Whatever happened must've been bad. She ran to the window. The policemen milling about in the street below were too close for comfort.

"What we need is a dog," she muttered. "A large dog!"

She wished Charlie was here. He would know what to do. *Damn him! Damn him for leaving Alex and me!* She buried her face in her hands and cried. The racking sobs left her body spent. She picked up the picture on the nightstand and held it close to her heart.

"I love you, Charlie," she whispered.

I love you, Charlie, mimicked back, cold and harsh, but the words went unnoticed amid the pounding of her heart.

She caressed the smiling face staring back at her from the photograph. Two years had passed since Charlie went away. His life had been snuffed out because some intoxicated old fool staggered into the path of his oncoming car. Charlie had swerved and lost control of his vehicle. There was nothing else he could've done, except run the man over. She swallowed a sob. God help her, she wished he'd mowed the man down. She hadn't even had a chance to say goodbye.

Alex was starting to ask questions to which she had no answers. Was her son so desperate to have a father figure in his life, he'd invented an imaginary male presence? She'd heard of such cases. But if that was true, why was he so afraid of this imaginary man?

She returned the photograph to its honorary place on the night table, touching a finger to her lips, then to the lips of the smiling face in the frame.

She moved to the window, noting that forensics had arrived on the scene. Mesmerized, she watched the figures in their ill-fitting suits scurrying around like a colony of red ants.

Cameras flashed like bolts of lightning, changing the gray morning sky into a surrealistic work of art. She shrugged and moved away, pausing to right the photograph lying face down on the nightstand.

She dressed quickly and slipped out the door, closing it softly behind her so as not to wake Alex. She twisted the doorknob, testing the lock, then ran down the stairs and slipped out onto the street, curious to see what all the commotion was about.

It had started to rain, a cold drizzle that soaked through to the bone. She shivered and folded her arms, seeking warmth from her body as she edged closer to the yellow tape sealing off the crime scene. She could see small numbered markers placed next to what looked like, from a distance, pieces of human remains. *Could she have slept through a bomb blast?*

She lifted the tape and stooped to slip underneath. Strong hands grabbed her from behind. A stern voice ordered her back. Before turning to face the beefy policeman, she caught a glimpse of what looked like a headless torso.

"What happened?" she stammered. "Please, officer, tell me what's going on. Is that—is it—"

Strong fingers closed around her arm and the officer steered her toward the entrance of her apartment building.

"There's been a murder, miss. That's all I can say."

Angel glanced back to see a black body bag being loaded into the coroner's van.

Inside, she stumbled blindly up the stairs. Reaching her floor, she fumbled with the lock. Her fingers refused to obey even the simplest commands. She looked back across her shoulder, fearful the murderer was going to pop around the corner and sprint up the stairs at any second. When the lock clicked, she stumbled inside and slammed the door shut. Her breath came in short gasps. She leaned heavily against the wall to keep her knees from buckling.

Clutching her chest, she staggered down the hall to check on Alex. She breathed a sigh of relief to find him sleeping peacefully. Something awful had happened yards from her front door! She made her way to the bathroom and splashed her face with cold water.

The screech of tires and an anguished cry sent her running out again. People had swarmed out of the apartments, rubbernecking, blocking her way. Children, lost in the crowd, screamed in terror at all the commotion, but no one seemed to care.

She elbowed her way past unshaven characters in wife beaters and boxer shorts and 'ladies' with curlers in their hair, treading cautiously around the unsavory punks and known crime offenders until she broke through and got a clear view of the street.

A milling crowd sidestepped a large black dog stretched out on the roadway, and the uniformed officers blatantly ignored its piteous crying.

She ducked under the restraining arm of the same beefy policeman who only minutes before had ordered her back. She ran toward the helpless creature and tried to avoid looking at the gruesome scene unfolding near her as the forensic people shoved body parts into plastic bags.

She winced as the policeman grabbed her arm and dug his fingers into her flesh.

"This is a crime scene, lady. Go back inside and lock your door. Slide the deadbolt into place and don't come out unless the building's on fire!"

She broke free and ducked under the yellow tape and ran toward the injured dog. She held her stomach, trying not to vomit as she stepped over pools of blood seeping from underneath the tarps, tinting the rainwater a pastel pink.

She knelt beside the whimpering animal, but firm hands lifted her bodily to her feet. She looked up into the eyes of two angry officers. Her eyes misted.

"Poor thing." Two large tears rolled down her cheeks. "Help me get him inside. Please."

She ran ahead as two burly officers lifted the injured dog and, laboring under its weight, puffed their way up the steep flight of stairs.

"Interfere again and it's off to jail, missy," declared the red-faced officer.

Angel smiled prettily as she practically shoved the officers out the door and turned her attention to the dog. Water seeped from his waterlogged fur and made a puddle on the floor. She hurried to fetch a towel. She returned to find the dog sitting on its haunches, dripping saliva off his tongue. He was a gargantuan specimen unlike any she had ever seen. The paw prints on her floor were the size of saucers and his head was massive. He was a gorgeous animal, but his eyes frightened her a bit. Intelligence lurked within their amber depths far beyond the comprehension of an average canine. This animal had obviously been trained, but for what?

"Well, look at you. Guess you must've just had the wind knocked out of you."

She held out her hand and let the dog sniff it. "Hope you're friendly, big fellow."

She sat down beside the dog and felt him over, but could find no injury. The dog licked her hand and laid his head in her lap, wagging his tail against the floor.

She stroked his head. "We're going to get along fabulously. Won't Alex be surprised?"

She stood, went to the cupboard, took down a plastic bowl and filled it with tap water, then rescued a half-eaten cheeseburger from the garbage can and tossed it on the floor in front of the dog.

The animal padded to the water bowl with a stealthy gait that belied his docile demeanor. He lapped a sip or two of the cold water, but edged away from the meat offering as if he found it distasteful.

Angel nudged the burger with her foot, shoving it closer to the dog. "Eat. The pickings are rather scarce around here."

The dog came to her and sniffed her crotch. She

laughed and pushed his head away.

"If you don't mind, we'll stick to a more socially accepted way of getting to know one another."

She stepped forward as Alex came into the room, dragging his raggedy blankie behind him. *God! If only she could find comfort in a flimsy piece of cloth!*

She forced a smile and pointed at the dog. "Look! Guess who's going to be living with us."

Alex hid behind her and wrapped his arms around her leg.

"Him bad."

She tousled his hair. "Good morning to you, Grumpy."

She moved into the kitchen, with Alex still attached to her leg. She managed to fill a bowl with cereal and poured a glass of orange juice.

"Remember, Alex, we talked about finding a dog? Well, this one found us."

"Him bad," Alex repeated.

Although Alex let go of her leg and sat at the table, she noticed her son kept an eye on the dog and pulled his feet up onto the chair. She ruffled Alex's hair and gave him a quick squeeze.

"You two will be good friends, you'll see."

She returned to the window and peered down the street below. There were more flashing lights and figures running hither and thither like cartoon characters than there were before.

The yellow tape had been extended closer to her building, which indicated something had been found even nearer than she had first thought. She stepped from the window and said a prayer, thankful to be on the second floor. It made her feel disconnected from the street below, even though her tiny apartment was located at the top of the stairs leading directly down to whatever evil might be lurking in the streets.

She picked up the telephone and checked for a dial tone. At the sound of the familiar buzz, she exhaled, emptying her lungs so forcefully, her chest caved in like a deflated balloon. She was undecided what to do next. She was afraid to unlock her door and venture outside, but she was even more afraid to remain home once the policemen had finished their work and gone away. She'd always heard that a murderer returned to the scene of the crime. According to the bits of news she'd managed to catch while Alex was eating his breakfast, this crime showed signs of being the work of a serial killer.

She picked Alex up and wrapped her arms around him as if this act of love would shield her child from the ugliness of the world outside. She shuddered at the thought of letting her darling baby boy out of her arms for even a moment, but she had to tighten security measures in the apartment. She needed deadbolts, lots of deadbolts. Did she dare risk dragging Alex around the city with a psychopathic killer on the loose?

Trembling, she dialed a taxicab and waited. Something wet and moist touched her hand and she screamed. Alex buried his face against her neck and started to cry.

The dog! She wondered what twist of fate had sent him to her. Was he a blessing from God…a guardian angel perhaps? Maybe he'd lost his way and was simply at the wrong place at the right time. It didn't matter. She wasn't going to let him go, ever.

The distinctive sound of a car horn announced the arrival of her taxi. She put down food and water for the dog and ran down the stairs with Alex on her hip and the shadow of a smile on her lips.

CHAPTER SIX

Garmin stretched leisurely. A pleasurable sigh passed his lips. It felt good to straighten his body. He watched the woman hurry toward the taxicab as she struggled to balance an oversized bag on her shoulder and keep the whimpering child from slipping off her rounded hip. The little snot-nosed brat was going to pose a problem. He could feel it deep down in his gut. The situation needed to be remedied and soon! A subtle smile crossed his face. He was very adept at dealing with small yummy boys.

He peered up and down the street before stepping out of the building. The rain was coming down hard, but the dismal conditions did not discourage him in the least. Water washed over him like a fountain as he assessed the neighborhood.

The noise made his head spin. The vroom, honking and wailing of an endless flow of traffic and music blasting from ever motorcar, doorway and street corner was deafening. The air was filled with loud, assertive voices as masses of people hurried along shoulder to shoulder but seemingly unaware of one another.

The putrid smell of urine stung his nostrils, but the stench of rotting garbage reminded him a little of the Styx River that wound around the underworld and served as a boundary between his world and the world of the living.

Working girls peddled their stuff on the street, taking shelter under leaky umbrellas. Gangs of young hooligans gathered under storefront awnings, tossing dice on the pavement and harassing passersby. Naked-butt children stared from the doorway of stairwells waiting for a chance to splash in puddles forming in sidewalk cracks.

His lips curled. There was nothing neighborly about this impoverished district of the city. The hood was a more apt description. The lady of his desire was much too fine to live in such dilapidated conditions. He intended to take her away from here, set her up in a castle, clothe her in the finest gowns, and lavish her with diamonds and jewels. She would want for nothing, except the boy.

Divide and conquer had worked well in the past when he found himself outnumbered in a delicate situation, but he sensed this technique would not work with this woman.

He didn't understand the bond between the woman and the boy, but he would allow her to play the mommy game for a while longer. It amused him. But there was no place for the boy in his domain. When his patience waned, he would simply take the woman and leave this forsaken place and the boy behind.

A plan was taking shape in his mind. The ingeniousness of his plot sent tingles of excitement up his spine. He chuckled.

"Love's the key."

The woman would fall for it. He just had to tweak the right buttons. He would enjoy watching her struggle against temptation of the flesh. His plan was infallible. In the end, she'd give in to love and he to his lust, satisfying both their needs. When he asked the all-consuming question, the woman would jump into his arms in unconditional surrender, ripe and ready for picking. No more Alex!

She might feel a small sense of guilt, maybe even re-morse, at leaving the child behind, but those feelings would pass. He hoped she would not let the past inter-fere with their new beginning.

A frown creased his brow. It might be wise to elimi-nate the problem before a conflict arose...an accident perhaps. Accidents happened every day. If such drastic measures became necessary, he'd be there to comfort the woman in her time of sorrow, be her pillar of strength and wipe away her tears. He howled gleefully. His brain was riddled with the many wonderfully wicked possibili-ties to rid the woman of the parasite she called Alex, without arousing suspicion.

He would implement his plan soon and see how things progressed. He laughed. After all, he did have a foot in the door, which put him a step ahead of the competition. He would've liked to have scored higher in the local social pecking order, but he'd given the woman what she wanted, and it appeared to be working out in his favor. A sardonic smile creased his face. One should be careful for what one wished.

****

Garmin's attention was drawn to a straggly figure standing on the street corner shouting, "Extra! Extra! Read all about it. Crazed maniac claims another victim."

His long strides closed the gap between him and the boy. He snatched the printed pages from the grubby fin-gers of the newspaper boy and quickly scanned the head-lines. He paid no heed to the boy's high-pitched voice or the tug on his shirt as the youth shouted excitedly, "One dollar, sir, one dollar."

He knocked the stack of newspapers to the sidewalk with a backward sweep of his hand.

"Lies! All lies!"

He bared his teeth and snarled ferociously. The paperboy screamed and ran off. Garmin tensed, ready to give chase, but his eye caught a familiar scene playing in a flashing box inside a plate glass window. His finger streaked the glass, tracing the movements of the tiny people scurrying about like beetles. A voice coming out of the box was talking about the same crazed lunatic that had the imbecile boy so excited. How dare these spineless creatures spread such rubbish! Garmin Maximilian was not about to allow some *crazed maniac* to claim credit for his night's activities. He'd hunt the shameful creature down and have a serious conversation about poaching someone's score.

Anger triggered a geyser of adrenaline so intense it awakened the sleeping beast inside him and stimulated his ravenous appetite. He was fully aware that to step outside the shadow of darkness to stalk prey put his well thought out strategy regarding the woman at risk. He would need to be extra careful and more inventive on this hunt.

He lifted his head and inhaled deeply. Fresh meat! He stepped back and leaned against the wall of a building that a flashing sign proclaimed to be Big Dave's Tattoo Shop. His ears perked to a thunderous roar. He remained motionless as a shiny, black and chrome motorcycle roared to a stop directly in front of the shop a few feet from where he stood. He had seen these two-wheel contraptions before in the crystal skull, but they were much more powerful and louder than he imagined. A caustic odor burned his eyes and made his nostrils quiver. He waited impatiently as the rider planted both feet on the pavement, revved the motor, then allowed it to settle down to a mellow purr.

His nerve endings were sparks of electricity as the rider removed his helmet and finger-combed strands of greasy hair. The man was big. *Badass* was written above the knuckles on each hand, and a joint of tobacco weed dangled from his lips. The jagged scar running down his cheek and the pictures of death smeared on his skin suggested he would not be easy prey.

Finally, a worthy opponent! Garmin stepped away from the building.

"Hey, Bro, nice Har…ley," he said in the native guttural language, reading the name on the machine. "Too nice for a corpulent bastard like you."

He watched the man's eyes narrow and the face go red. As the rider stepped away from the machine, Garmin could see in the depths of the man's eyes he was confident in his ability to annihilate the insolent stranger.

Garmin backed away a few steps.

"Make like the north wind and blow me, you bow-legged jackass."

Tingles ran up Garmin's spine as the man plucked a heavy chain from a bag hanging on the machine and advanced toward him. He ran down the street, staying just ahead of the man pursuing him. He stopped in front of a street sign that read, Eight Ball Alley, and gave the man a one-finger salute.

The man lunged at him, but Garmin darted into the alley and quickly disappeared from sight. The occasional clang as he made contact with a tin can or whiskey bottle made it easy for the man to follow.

He embraced the shadows and waited. The man passed by so closely, Garmin could feel his breath hot on his face. He snickered as the burly figure stalked past him, muttering obscenities. He cleared his throat noisily and stepped out of his hiding place, crouching low to the pavement.

"Looking for me?"

The man wheeled around and peered at him in the dim light. His expression changed from anger to shocked disbelief.

"What the hell!"

Garmin motioned him forward. "Show me what you've got, big boy." He allowed the man to swing, taking the full brunt of a smashing blow to his face, followed by several more to his midriff without as much as a grunt.

"My turn," he said.

He extended his left arm and placed his palm against the man's forehead and held him.

"Play time! You hide and I'll seek."

He followed as the man fled down the alley, filled with loathing. From the look and size of the Harley rider, he had expected one hell of a fight. This was big game: intelligent, aggressive, and capable of evasive maneuvers that could turn the hunter into the hunted, but the man was scared shitless and running like a jackrabbit.

His loathing turned to anger. The excitement of the chase was gone. The game was over almost before it began. He was ashamed to call it a hunt, more like easy pickings. Yet, the thrill of the kill would be sweet regardless of the unworthiness of the prey.

His nostrils twitched.

"Ready or not, here I come!"

He stood in front of the crouched form cowering underneath a piece of corrugated paper. He snatched the cardboard from the man's hands.

"Tag!" Garmin muttered and unsheathed his claws.

"Oh, my God!" the man whispered hoarsely.

Garmin's upper lips flared as his canines dropped. He stared down at the pathetic creature, focusing on the man's round, black, terror-glazed eyes. His pulse quickened.

"Please don't hurt me!" screamed the man.

Garmin's right hand clamped around the thick neck and lifted the man off the pavement. He held the struggling figure aloft, amazed at the length of the man's protruding tongue. His left hand stabbed, plowed through the chest cavity, found the heart and ripped it out.

The quivering mass lay in his hand. Thump! Thump! Thump! He touched the heart, tracing the intricate vein patterns with his finger. The hair on the back of his neck bristled and his own heart pounded.

"Ahhhh!"

He licked the cone-shaped ambrosial delicacy and found it delightful. He devoured the organ, savoring the last morsel, feeling sorrowful when it was gone.

He beat his chest and howled in agony and jubilation as he was broadsided with simultaneous bursts of emotion. The man had known sorrow and pain, great joy and freedom...something Garmin had never experienced. Recklessness kindled inside him. In his calculated world, such feelings would prove disastrous, but he could feel his vigor returning and had a sudden desire to feel the wind on his face.

He gazed into the vacant eyes of the corpse and poked it with his finger. A grinning skull, with a snake crawling out its eyeball, stared up from a tattered T-shirt.

"The Maiden and the snake pit," he muttered. "All the amenities of home."

Was this a premonition of what awaited him at the end of his return journey? He pulled the leather vest together to cover the face on the man's shirt. This place reeked of bad karma.

He retraced his footsteps along the path he had come, ending at the woman's apartment building. He climbed the stairs, removed the paper wad from the latch and slipped through the door. No need for special effects when a simple trick of the trade would suffice.

Inside, he drank a cold glass of water, changed, and made himself comfortable on the sofa to wait.

"Let the games begin," he muttered. "Let the games begin."

CHAPTER SEVEN

The glare of streetlights cast dark shadows against the graffiti covered walls, and the wail of police sirens boded ill for some poor unfortunate soul as Angel stepped out of the taxicab, entered the building and climbed the stairs. Her ascent was hindered by the child draped across her shoulder. Alex was getting to be just about more than she could carry.

In front of her door, she fumbled to insert the key into the lock. Had the murderer struck again? Was he lurking in the shadows, watching and waiting for a chance to snatch her and Alex?

She threw the house keys on the table and deposited the boy on his bed. A hint of an indulgent smile tugged at the corners of her mouth. The wee thing was out like a light, the sleep of the innocent. She'd never be able to sleep soundly like that again. The humanity's psycho-pathic dribble made peaceful sleep impossible. Thinking about the gruesome scene this morning, she couldn't understand how anybody could be so twisted. The police were keeping a lot of the grizzly details close to the vest, but she'd witnessed the scattered body parts first hand when she'd defied the hand of authority and ran to aid a poor helpless animal left to die in the rain-drenched street.

She backed against the wall. Her arms automatically shielded her face as a dark figure uncurled from the shadows. She laughed hysterically.

"It's you!"

She dropped to her knees and threw her arms around

the neck of the horrendous black dog, burying her face in the soft fur, then sprang to her feet.

"Oh, my goodness! You've been penned up all these hours."

She threw open the tiny closet and snatched out a thick leather belt, not caring if it was her favorite accessory. She slipped it in place, only to discover the belt was a few inches shy of the diameter of the dog's monstrous neck. She ran into the bedroom and came back with Charlie's belt. To her surprise, the thirty-two inch belt fit perfectly. Shaking her head in disbelief, she retrieved the belt from her terry bathrobe, threaded it underneath the makeshift collar and knotted it securely.

"Good."

She scratched behind the dog's ears. "Hope you don't decide to chase a car or a cat, big guy."

She knew she couldn't do it even as she tugged on the makeshift leash. She tried to force her feet to move toward the door, but her knees were trembling so badly, she could barely stand. *No way!* She was fooling herself. She was too frightened to go out into the night, not even with what she guessed to be two hundred pounds of teeth and muscle at her side. Besides, she couldn't leave Alex asleep while she walked the dog.

She knelt. Her fingers groped the thick fur, undid the collar and allowed it to fall to the floor. Moving quickly before she lost her nerve, she slid the deadbolt open and eased the door wide enough to let the dog pass.

"You're free, boy. Go with God."

The hair bristled on the dog's back and a deep growl rumbled in his throat. Angel opened the door wider.

"Go!"

The dog trotted out. She slammed the door shut and leaned against it, too terrified to move as fierce angry barks echoed in the narrow encasement of the stairwell. *Something was out there!*

She pressed her face against the door, pleading for the dog to come back. The silence was deafening. He had disappeared into the night. His presence had provided her a sense of security, but it was too late. He was gone when she needed him most.

She covered her ears with her hands. God! She wished that incisive noise would stop. She moved toward the phone, her eyes transfixed on the shiny black surface. Her hand hovered over the instrument. Each ring sent tiny shock waves through her body like jolts of electrical current. Fear crawled through her guts. She sucked in deep breaths and exhaled slowly until her heart dropped to a more normal rhythm.

"It isn't as if the gory hand of fate can reach out of the blasted telephone."

The words did not provide any measure of comfort. From what she'd seen, it wasn't hands that had done the damage. It appeared more like tooth and nail. The murderer was a savage beast.

The fact that the victim was torn to pieces practically on her doorstep had her nerves jingling. She was in the wake of destruction. Her *child* was in the wake of destruction.

She snatched the instrument from its cradle.

"Hello," she whispered.

The resounding click told her the caller was no longer on the line. She held the telephone against her ear and started to cry. What if *she* had come to a bad end instead of that poor man? Who would know or care? Hatcheck girls were a dime a dozen. Nobody would come looking if she didn't show up for work. What would happen to Alex?

She dropped the instrument as though it burned her hand. The handset dangled off the table, rotating as the coiled cord unwound, swinging back and forth.

She stumbled across the room and collapsed onto a chair. The hair on her neck stood at attention. There *was* something out there. She could feel it in every fiber of her being. She ran to the kitchen and grabbed a butcher knife off the counter. Let the dirty bastard come. Angel McKeough wasn't going down without a fight! She'd defend her child until the last drop of blood drained from her body.

She dragged the shabby old sofa across the floor, blocking the entrance to Alex's room. She dropped the knife and fell down on her knees and prayed. She prayed for the poor dog she'd turned loose on the wicked city streets, prayed for strength, prayed to die bravely, and prayed that Alex wouldn't suffer. She could feel her heart palpitating. Her voice was scarcely audible as she struggled to catch her breath. She prayed that God was listening, and prayed for the tortured soul of the man who felt the need to inflict pain and suffering onto his fellow men.

She picked up the knife and pulled her tired body onto the couch. She hugged a grungy little teddy bear tightly against her bosom and started to sing Alex's favorite lullaby. The words slurred, becoming indistinguishable. Sleep blanketed her body, wrapping her up and tucking her in snugly for a brief moment in time as if her body was trying to prevent her brain from short-circuiting.

A faint sound penetrated her deep REM, bringing her back to a conscious state. She sat up and listened, her body cold and stiff with fear. It came again, the distinct squeak of the twelfth stair step.

Clutching the knife, she leapt to her feet and tiptoed to the door, pressing her ear hard against it as she strained to catch the slightest sound. Heavy breathing and distinctive scuffling near the door left no doubt something was lurking outside.

One swift kick was all it would take to splinter the wood and spring the door open.

"Come on, you murderous scum of the earth!" she shouted. "Do what you came to do. You can't kill someone who's already dead!"

The knife slipped through her numb fingers and clattered to the floor. She hadn't realized until that moment the truth of her words. She'd gone through the motions of living since Charlie went away, but she was as dead inside as his body now molding in the ground. For the first time in two years, Angel cared whether she lived or died. She no longer wanted to be with Charlie in the afterlife; she wanted to live for Alex.

She sank, closed her eyes and drew her legs up, hugging her knees against her chin. Her body started to sway. She smiled and opened her eyes, but she was no longer in the now. She was safe in her little princess canopy bed as Mama read her a favorite bedtime story where good always triumphed over evil. Her world was pink and rosy and dolly was sitting beside her, listening.

Angel blinked and suddenly, she was all grown up,

seeing herself watching nervously out the window, listening for the familiar roar of Charlie's old Chevy. She hoped he wouldn't think the bright red prom dress with a sprinkling of rhinestones was too gaudy. She giggled and adjusted the neckline to reveal as much cleavage as the bra could push upward, and pulled her fake fur stole across her chest until she could make her escape from the watchful eyes of Mama and Daddy.

Another flash in time and she was marching down the aisle clutching Daddy's arm, smiling happily as he handed her off to Charlie. She felt Charlie's kiss on her lips, soft at first, then practically scandalous, as his mouth claimed his bride in a lubricious display of passion.

Alex cried out in his sleep, clearing away the fog of yesterdays, bringing her back to a place in time where there did not seem to be a happy ever after.

"Sometimes in the real world, the bad guys win," she whispered hoarsely. She jumped at the faint scratching sound on the other side of the door. It came again, louder, followed by a low whine.

"Thank you, Jesus."

She flung the door open, forgetting that a short time before, she'd been cowering on the floor fearful for her life.

"Oh, you wonderful, beautiful beast!"

She dropped to her knees and squeezed the dog so tightly, he yelped with righteous indignation. She let him go and rushed into the kitchen to set out some food and water. He declined the offering and trotted off to take up residency on the sofa.

If he'd been human, she would have sworn his eyes

registered disappointment because she didn't sit beside him.

She struggled under the extra weight as she dragged the sofa to its original position.

"It's been one hell of an evening, boy, but since you're here, I'm going to bed."

She kissed the dog's wet nose and was rewarded with a slobbering slick tongue across the lips.

Sleep didn't come easy. Angel wondered if she'd experienced a breakdown of some sort, or if the flashbacks were a near death experience.

"Charlie…"

With her husband's name on her lips, she slowly sank into a restless slumber.

****

The faint aroma of pipe tobacco and the familiar smell of cologne pricked the depth of her subconscious, Charlie's favorite brand. She stirred and moaned softly as firm lips closed on hers, then trailed down her neck, lingering on her most sensitive spot before sliding down to her breasts.

"Oh, Charlie, I dreamed you had died," she whispered.

What a nightmare! Thank God Charlie was safe and sound, sleeping beside her in his own bed…their bed. She giggled softly. Well, not exactly sleeping. She struggled against the flimsy fabric of her nightgown, exposing her naked breast to the searing advances of his hot lips. Her nipples stood shamelessly erect. She whimpered with desire as his tongue teased her breast, then cupped the areola and drew it inside his mouth. She moaned softly as he suckled her breast.

She could feel his arousal pulsating through the rough fabric of his trousers. Her body trembled as the throbbing between her thighs intensified. Pleasure juice ran down the crevices of her rounded buttocks like melted butter.

She guided his hand to her wetness, digging her nails deep into his flesh as he found her pleasure button. Waves of unadulterated ecstasy made her body quiver as he slid a finger inside her, but she wanted more. She wanted to feel his cock buried deep inside her, transcend earthly bonds and come together in a celestial nova, one body, one heart, and one soul.

She struggled to undo the zipper of his trousers, but it refused to yield to her trembling fingers. *Why in the hell was Charlie sleeping in those damn things?* Her fingers traced the outline of the bulge inside his pants. *God! He was a stud horse!*

"Charlie!" She giggled. "What big balls you have."

Her tongue probed his lips and wiggled its way into the recesses of his mouth. She rolled over and pressed against him, rubbing her slick pussy against the pulsating bulb straining to break free from the restraining confines of his trousers. Rhythmic spasms of raw passion carried her to the edge, but her body was demanding his rock-hard member to take her over the rim, through the cosmos and to the stars. She begged him to take her, pleading like an addict in need of a fix.

His breath was hot against her skin. "All in good time," he whispered softly. "All in good time."

Then he was gone, swallowed up in the blackness of the night, or the depths of her mind?

She sat up and turned on the bedside lamp. Nothing stirred in the solitary silence of the room.

"No!" she screamed. "Don't leave me, Charlie. Please, God, don't take him from me again."

Blood seeped through her fingers and dripped onto the sheets as her nails buried into her palms. She sucked in a sharp breath. There was an indentation on the opposite bed pillow! Shaking with trepidation, she stretched out her hand, startled to discover the pillow felt warm to the touch.

"Charlie," she whispered, "am I losing my mind?"

Footsteps padded across the floor. A dark figure climbed into bed beside her and rested his head on the pillow. She gasped. "The damn dog!"

She shoved the animal hard, but he didn't budge. She buried her face in his fur, sobbing hysterically. "Why couldn't you have been Charlie?" *Now, she was talking to a dog!*

She stumbled out of bed and kicked the crumpled nightdress under the bed. She *never* wanted to see that thing again. Not bothering to robe, she plodded to the bathroom. She snatched a couple of towels off the shelf and turned the shower on full blast, cold. She scrubbed until her arms ached. The water cascaded down her face, but the icy stream drenching her body had little effect on the emotional tide that had shattered her dreams.

Angel was surprised to see the dog had followed her. He lay beside the shower watching as she toweled off. She slipped on a bathrobe and drew the belt tightly around her. Something about his eyes made her flesh crawl. His eyes looked almost human. She snatched a hairbrush off the sink basin and hurried into the living room. She paced the floor. The dog followed, nosing her crack. She opened the door.

"Go!"

The slamming door awakened Alex. He raised his arms to be lifted and clung to her neck.

He whimpered. "Man bad. Alex not like man."

She held him tightly. "Did you have another nightmare, sweetheart? Mommy won't let any old man hurt her baby."

"The man hates Alex," he whispered, "but him likes Mommy."

She laid Alex down on the bed and knelt beside him. She cupped his face in her hands.

"Baby, where in the world did you come up with that idea?"

"Man said," Alex replied. "Man comes when Mommy sleeps. Man said Alex better keep his mouth shut and stay out of the way."

"It's only a dream, baby. Mommy had a bad dream, too. Now let's forget all about it and eat our breakfast."

She filled the cereal bowls and poured the juice. Her thoughts ran rampant and queasiness pressed against her abdominal wall. This was not the first time Alex had referred to *The Man*. But there wasn't any man, just Alex, her, and the dog.

The latch was still locked. No one could have slipped the deadbolt back into place on his way out. Alex must have picked up on her anxieties, or else, he'd seen or heard something on the television about the murder. He was too young to understand, but some of the news flashes were graphic. Poor little guy. No wonder he was having bad dreams.

A loud bark announced the return of the dog she'd callously thrown outside. She felt somewhat remorseful and more than a little silly. His size was a bit daunting, but the big dog was just what Alex and she needed with a murderer loose in the streets. She really must give the creature a name. It wasn't right to keep calling it Dog. She opened the door and let him inside. He trotted to Alex and reared up on the table beside his chair with his tongue hanging out, salivating.

Alex turned his juice over and started to cry. The shrill shrieks grated on Angel's already frazzled nerves like raking fingernails across a chalkboard.

"Hush, Alex!" she said a bit too firmly, causing him to scream even louder.

She picked him up and carried him to the couch. The dog was spread out over half its length. Angel pushed on the creature's hindquarters and plopped Alex down beside it.

"Make room, dog."

He screamed louder. She tried to cuddle him, but the child's body was rigid. After what seemed like an eternity, his screams subsided to sniffles, and she was shocked to discover he'd wet his pants.

Her eyes filled with tears. She'd been through hell during the past twenty-four hours. It didn't look as though the day was going to get any better. She curled on the sofa and cuddled Alex close to her bosom. She yawned sleepily, buried her toes in the dog's warm fur and fell back to sleep.

She awoke with a start. She'd slept well into the afternoon. If she hurried, she might have time to catch a cup of coffee at *Marvin's All Night Diner*, located next door to *Club Venus*. A hatcheck girl at a gentlemen's club was not a profession she would have chosen had she been given a choice, but she'd been desperate and couldn't find anything better. It was steady work, paid the rent, and kept her respectable, which was more than could be said for about ninety-five percent of the tenants in her miserable apartment building.

She poured a double shot of bourbon and gulped it down straight, gasping as the fiery liquid made contact with her stomach. She downed a second shot, and another. She wasn't a drinker, but tonight, she needed the liquid courage the whiskey provided.

She dressed hurriedly and dialed *Yellow Stripe Cab Service*. She struggled to balance Alex on her hip as she poured another shot of bourbon and waited impatiently for the telltale blast of the cabbie's horn.

CHAPTER EIGHT

Angel hated like hell going to work. After the sensuous, hallucinatory experience a few hours earlier, the thought of spending the next eight to ten hours confined inside four walls with hard peckers and hot pussies made her so horny, she was on the brink of grabbing the first thing with a bulge and having her way with him.

She'd remained celibate for the past two years. There had been ample opportunities to become involved with respectable men, and some not so respectable, but she had no desire to share her heart or her bed. She felt as if she'd be cheating, but her body had turned against her. Instead of a holy temple, her body was more like a cross-cut saw. She was so aroused it would definitely take two men to handle her.

This eruption of lascivious cravings was a totally new experience. Night after night, she'd seen men getting their rocks off as half-naked showgirls provided lap rocket overhauls, doing anything for a buck. She'd not felt the slightest flicker of desire watching this live action, yet, an erotic dream had her climbing the walls. She supposed it was because the dream had ended just short of orgasm. God! She'd been so close and it had felt so good!

She had to figure out what had triggered these rogue emotions and deal with it. Alex was the only man in her life and she intended to keep it that way. Men were dogs! She already had a dog, a very large dog. She should be thankful instead of pissing and moaning about some dream lover that didn't have the balls to finish what he'd started.

"Ahhhh!" Those balls had been huge!

"Focus, girl," she mumbled and forced her mind back on the dog. A dog was man's best friend, and a woman's, and a much more reliable bedfellow than some imaginary stud muffin.

Perhaps she'd give some thought to a relationship if the right man came along, but she wasn't about to rush into anything no matter how strong her cravings. That's exactly what it was, a craving. Her body had been asleep these two years and had wakened hungry.

She laughed aloud at her brilliant conclusion, causing the cabbie to glance at her suspiciously through the rear view mirror. She giggled again. If he knew what was going through her mind, he'd really freak out.

A cab was a necessary inconvenience until she could afford her own car. She'd loved the leisurely drives through the country, sitting next to Charlie. After three glorious years of marriage, Charlie and she still liked to sneak off to a secluded spot every now and then, spread a blanket and made love like a couple of teenagers. It was a memory she'd always treasure and was the one thing that had kept her sane since his passing.

She burped loudly. The regurgitated liquor vapors stung her nostrils and filled the car with a nauseating stench. Charlie would be disappointed. He would want her to move on with her life, but he'd be sorely troubled to see her slip from a respectable lady to a common whore ready to lie down and spread her legs for anybody who could scratch her itch.

She'd even given the cabbie a second look before deciding some principles just couldn't be compromised.

The rancid stench of the man's breath made her dry heave. The bastard must've had sardines for dinner the prior evening. Besides, if she didn't miss her guess, the man was a rabbit fucker. She'd end up hotter when he finished than she was before he started. A rabbit was not what she had in mind for her sexual debut. She was going after big game.

The first time around had been for love. It had gotten her nowhere. She felt a stab of guilt. She shouldn't be bitter. Charlie had been the victim. He hadn't asked to be taken out of her life, but she was angry with him for leaving her.

The tragic accident had taken the good and left the bad. God must have been taking a nap! The minister had told her it was a part of God's plan and Charlie was in a far better place. She hadn't believed him then, and she didn't believe him now. Charlie's place was at her side, helping raise their son.

She'd lost everything: her home, car, and her life's companion. Pent-up rage churned inside her like molten lava. She'd lost it all by foul play and, by hell, she'd get it back the same way. She'd find some well-heeled old geezer and play him like a fiddle.

The club was full of potential candidates. She'd just have to keep her eyes open. The older the better. She'd fuck the old fart into oblivion. She giggled. She was turning into a cold calculating bitch. She wasn't proud of the fact, but she had to think of Alex.

She'd do whatever it took, short of peddling her ass on the street to see that her son had every opportunity life had to offer. If it meant auctioning her body to the highest bidder, she'd do it, but she'd demand a ring on her finger to seal the bargain, and no prenuptial agreement to foil the works.

She undid the top button of her blouse, then a second and a third. If she wanted to reel in the big fish, she'd have to use the right bait.

A woman alone had to use whatever assets she had to gain the upper hand in a man's world. Clearly, her body was her best asset, but it was divided against itself. The temptations of the flesh were too strong to resist. She'd end up giving in sooner or later, so why not turn the inevitable to her advantage? She loved the simplicity of her plan.

She rummaged through her purse, found her favorite perfume, and sprayed a strong blast to the pulse points. She laughed as the cabbie sniffed the air and rolled down the window. The bastard would be well advised to take advantage of the sweet fragrance. He reeked.

She'd noticed the driver watching her from the rearview mirror, and could see the perfume was affecting him severely. She'd bet a dollar to a nickel he would shoot a load into his shorts before she reached her destination. Amen to him! He wasn't going to poke his stubby little nubbin inside her. The way his stomach protruded, she doubted he could even find the damn thing. Screwing that fat bastard would be like fucking a basketball.

She closed her eyes and pretended to sleep. She had a long night ahead of her. Maybe she'd get lucky and score a direct hit right out of the dugout. She was willing if some wealthy old fart was able. The sitter would be happy to keep Alex overnight for a few extra bucks.

She fired up a cigarette and blew smoke rings that

spiraled upward and dissipated into nothingness.

"Just like my life," she said, bitterly. "Spiraling out of control and going nowhere."

She felt Alex stir restlessly in the seat beside her. She hoped he wasn't going to start about *The Man* again. She was about to have man problems even more scary than the man in her son's nightmares.

She shuddered at the thought of some old withered up prune dick slobbering all over her while he tried to get his limp pecker hard enough to penetrate. But if he met her criteria for husband material and signed on the dotted line, she'd hold his damn thing inside her pussy with her bare hands until he dribbled its load, and she'd scream like he'd rocked her world.

She buried her face in her hands. What would Charlie think if he was watching her from wherever he was? He was a good man, so she assumed he was in heaven. What in the fuck was happening to her? And the language! She used to blush if Charlie said shit. Now, she dropped the F-bomb every time she opened her mouth.

She dabbed at the corners of her lips with the tip of her thumb and index finger, applied a heavy coat of lipstick, and fluffed her hair. If she expected to get out of hell, she'd have to sacrifice a few principles, come down off her high pedestal, and dance with the devil.

She still had some decency left. She had no intentions to defraud anybody. An old man married a much younger woman for two things: arm decoration and pussy, with the emphasis on pussy. She'd give the old guy what he wanted, two, three, four times a day. If he couldn't get it up, she'd get him off one way or another. A woman needed to please her man. She laughed. The action left a brassy taste in her mouth.

She'd play fair and treat the limp-dick old coffin-dodger with respect for however long he lasted. Once death did them part, she'd give him a proper sendoff, complete with a black dress and veil like any other grieving widow before grabbing the money and catching the first plane heading south.

Her thoughts drifted back to her dream, nightmare, or whatever way best described the horrid thing. Color flooded her face and her nipples hardened and pressed against the silky softness of her blouse. She squirmed on her seat and fought against the pleasurable ripples as her underwear rubbed against her crotch. She started to cream and could feel the wetness soaking through her panties. That's all she needed, to go to work smelling like a sardine can!

She tried to figure out what had inspired the dream. If it was something she'd eaten, she'd buy a whole damn bushel of the stuff. The dream had hit her like she'd been sandbagged. At least, she knew her feminine parts were still in working order, a good thing to know when a gal was on the prowl.

She told herself the dream was probably a reaction to all the stress and anxiety from the horror of a murder so close to her apartment building. She'd felt so alone and vulnerable. Now that the dog had appeared on the scene, things should get better.

The cab screeched to a halt in front of the babysitter's apartment. Angel could sense the driver's eyes raping her as she carried Alex up the walkway. With Alex taken care of, she returned to the taxi. She huddled in the corner of her seat and rummaged through her purse in search of a defense weapon, thankful to find a nail file buried underneath the contents of her makeup bag.

Her stomach knotted as the cabbie placed a flabby arm across the back of the seat and smiled at her over his shoulder. The man was about as subtle as a chainsaw. Yellow teeth, coated with a week's worth of groceries, practically popped out of his mouth. She shuddered and moved as far back in the seat as possible.

"Lovely evening, Madam," he said, noisily clearing his throat. "Nice view."

Angel could feel his eyes boring through her clothes. *This jackass had some nerve!* She looked away and remained silent. A sigh of relief blew through her lips as the taxi pulled away from the curb.

"Step on it," she said curtly. "I can't afford to be late."

She pretended not to notice the driver's left eye blinking at her through the rearview mirror like an erratic turn signal.

"Oh, we'll get there, Missy, and on time, too. I've been doing this a long time, and I know my way around pretty damn good. Know what I mean?"

She glared at him and turned to stare out the window, but the man refused to take the hint. Her stomach knotted as the driver twisted his head and leered at her exposed cleavage.

"I'm *real* good at reading signs."

She didn't answer. She clutched the nail file tightly between the fingers and fumbled with the three buttons on her blouse with her left hand.

The flashing billboard in the distance signaled her journey was coming to an end. *Thank God!* She ran a comb through her hair, tossed some bills onto the front seat and opened the door of the taxi before it came to a complete stop.

"Have a good night," she said sarcastically and hurried inside the club without a backward glance. She hesitated a moment, undid the top buttons on her blouse once again, and braced herself for the night ahead.

CHAPTER NINE

There was something vaguely familiar about the tall, dark man standing in front of her, although Angel was certain she'd never met him before. She would've remembered him.

She drew her bottom lip in under her teeth. A red stain leaked through the faint shadow of lipstick still remaining after four hours and seven cups of strong black coffee. A faint fluttering of her heart stirred feelings she thought had died with Charlie. She closed her eyes, remembering the taste of his beloved lips, the feel of his body pressed against her own, and his hands touching her in all the places she wanted to be touched. She missed him so!

Charlie had been a good lover, thoughtful and considerate of her needs. She told herself she would prefer tenderness and love over raw passionate sex every time, but she knew she was a liar. As much as she loved Charlie, their lovemaking had not even come close to the ecstasy she'd experienced during her erotic dream sex, and she hadn't even achieved the big 'O'.

She gave a guilty start as the man cleared his throat. He reached out and gently touched her lip.

"You're bleeding."

She gasped as he placed his finger in his mouth and sucked the red stain.

He touched her lip again. "There, I've made it all better."

Angel wrinkled her nose.

"Eeeew! Aren't you afraid you'll catch something

tasting other people's blood?"

Every nerve ending in her body tingled with excitement when the man smiled, flashing perfectly even white teeth.

"Not from a sweet little thing like you."

Her hands trembled as she needlessly shuffled stacks of paper from one pile to another.

"What can I do for you, sir? I...er...I don't see anything that needs to be checked."

"Oh, if we put our heads together, I'm sure we could think of something," he said. "If it'll buy me a few more moments of your time, you can check this."

She reached out and plucked the string tie dangling from the man's fingers. A pleasingly old-fashioned blush stained her cheeks as his eyes scanned her body with x-ray precision. She lowered her eyes and refused to meet his gaze.

"The action's inside."

He appeared to find the flushed cheeks quite charming.

"I kinda like the action out here."

She opened her mouth to speak, but the gentleman winked and moved inside the club, and was immediately swarmed by a horde of showgirls. The sound of his deep laughter mingling with high-pitched giggles grated on her nerves.

"Bitches!"

The whole pack was circling the man like a bunch of vultures, waiting to jump his bones and pick him clean.

"It'll serve him right," Angel muttered, forgetting that only a moment before, she'd harbored thoughts along those same lines.

She felt a sense of satisfaction and something akin to pride when the man didn't linger long inside the club. She noted, even though he was a bit tight fisted with his money, the girls sighed with disappointment when he took his leave.

She held her breath as a couple of girls followed him into the lobby. It flattered her to see those marvelous amber eyes were focused solely on her, without even a glance in the *ladies'* direction.

She pretended not to notice the man watching her, but her heart was pounding. Her fingers purposely brushed his as she handed him the string tie. Small electrical shock waves surged through her body, all directed at her heart.

The sound of his voice startled her.

"This isn't really my scene," he said. "How about a cup of coffee after your shift?"

"I don't get off for another three hours," she stammered, "if I'm lucky."

If he asked again, she knew her answer would be yes. She held her breath, trying hard not to let her gaze drop below his waist.

"I'll wait," he said. "Meet me at the diner. It's close and public. Wouldn't want you to think a stranger was going to snatch you and ravage your bones or other more delectable parts of your anatomy."

Before the retort forming on her full lips had a chance to be heard, the man had ducked out the door and was swallowed by the night.

She stared after him. His words were innocent enough, but his eyes said things she wasn't prepared to hear. Her brain screamed *bad idea*, but her lips whispered,

Lucid Dreams

"Okay."

The man wasn't likely to show up anyway. He'd just been engaging in a little harmless flirtation. She'd met his kind before and brushed the midnight Romeos off without as much as a thought. She'd go just to prove her point that men were dogs looking for a place to hide their bone.

****

Angel saw him before she entered the restaurant. He was at a table for two, seated by the window with a clear view of the street. As she approached, she could see he'd taken the liberty to have a steaming cup of black coffee and a huge slice of chocolate pie waiting for her. A single red rose lay on the table next to the empty chair.

She smiled and he flashed dazzling white teeth in return, and moved to slide the chair out to seat her as if the dingy little diner was a five star restaurant. She allowed him this act of chivalry and tried to ignore the good-natured hoots from the regulars.

The man didn't seem to mind. In fact, he didn't even seem to notice. He appeared to only have eyes for her. His intense gaze made her a bit self-conscious.

Her eyes involuntarily shifted to his fingers, long...very long, and slender, with no wedding band. This man was no ordinary Joe, of that, she was certain. She jumped at the sound of his voice. Gooseflesh pricked her arms as he leaned forward close enough that his breath kissed her lips.

"My friends call me Madd," he said.

Angel laughed a little too loudly. She noted his

mouth curved upward at the corners, and he nodded his head ever so slightly as if replying to an unanswered question. Was he mocking her? If he'd intended to make a joke, she'd missed the punch line. However, the look in his eyes fueled smoldering embers of passion into a fiery furnace, effectively easing her sting of indignation.

She reached out and took his outstretched hand. His touch burned her flesh like a branding iron. She drew in her breath sharply and dropped her handbag. Madd and she simultaneously bent to retrieve it and their eyes connected. The intimacy of his gaze had her blushing like a schoolgirl. She sat upright, flustered to find he had followed her movement without breaking eye contact. His look had the effect of ice cubes sliding down her spine, followed by red-hot coals of fire. She swallowed hard and reached for her fork. It slid through her trembling fingers and fell to the floor.

"And you?" he asked.

She squirmed uncomfortably in her chair. "Huh?"

"Your name? What be your name, my lady?"

She giggled nervously. Mind games! She'd play for a while as long as he didn't get too kinky.

"Angel. You can call me Angel, kind sir."

He blinked and looked away. "An…gel. The divine messenger."

When he turned back toward her, she noted his facial features had shifted from warm playfulness to a burning intensity.

"Well, An…gel, your coffee is getting cold," he said, and swallowed a gulp of the steaming liquid in his cup.

She took a small sip and gasped. "How did you do that?" She flinched as he practically poured the rest of his coffee down his throat.

"Some like it hot," he said.

She took out her wallet and showed him photographs of Alex. Although he leaned toward her as if hanging on to every word, she had the feeling children made him uncomfortable. That could prove to be a major problem in their relationship. She sucked in her breath sharply. This was the second time she'd ever set eyes on this man, and already she was making future plans.

After tonight, she would probably never see him again. She certainly hoped that was not the case. Everything about him was perfect as if he had been made to order.

A small still voice whispered inside her head, *'maybe too perfect'*, but she wasn't listening. She'd found the perfect man once before when she met Charlie. Although Madd was as dark as Charlie was fair, his mannerism, charismatic charm, and infectious laugher could've been a direct replica of her late husband. She wanted to get to know him better.

She didn't resist when he took her hand and pressed it to his lips.

"The hour is late, even for an Angel. You must want to get home to your delightful son."

She pulled her hand away. "Well…yes…I must call a—"

She didn't know whether to be angry or relieved when he told her he'd already taken the liberty to hail a taxi to take her home. She reluctantly allowed him to slide her chair back while her brain struggled to think of a way to keep him with her a little longer.

The sound of his voice, soft and caressing, was spell-binding.

"I'd offer to claim the honor myself, but I doubt if you'd be comfortable on the back of my iron steed in that fabulous attire. However, the prospect does sound delightful."

She fiddled with her purse, tempted to climb onto the bitch seat of his motorcycle, wrap her arms around his magnificent body and throw caution to the wind.

She giggled. "I can't think of anything more exciting than to have a knight in shining armor sweep me off my feet and carry me off to a faraway castle to live happily ever after. But I suppose I'd better stick with the trusted old taxicab tonight."

She tensed when she spotted a Yellow Stripe taxi waiting at the curb, and then laughed happily when she saw a gray-haired gentleman behind the wheel.

"If that's my ride, the driver's a sweetheart."

She winced as Madd's fingers tightened around her arm. She stole a glance from underneath her lashes, amused to see his jaw clenched and his lips pressed together. *The man was jealous!*

As the taxicab pulled away, she looked back to see Madd straddle a Harley. She leaned out the window and yelled, "Bye", but her words were lost in the rumble of the engine as he whacked the throttle wide open and disappeared from sight, riding the rear wheel.

She sank down into the seat and instructed the driver to proceed to the sitter's house. Although happy, she just wanted to pick up Alex and go home.

She had a sense of being watched as she stepped from the taxi. Feeling foolish, she asked the driver to walk with her to the front door and wait while she collected Alex.

Preoccupied in thought, she caught her shoe heel in a break in the sidewalk and would have fallen except for the cabby's steady hand. He held her arm and escorted her over the rough patches of concrete. She thanked him immensely, and when they got to her apartment building, offered a generous gratuity for his acts of kindness.

She put Alex to bed straight away, fed and watered the dog, and brewed a cup of her special blended tea. She propped her feet up and sipped the concoction, letting the sweet aroma of jasmine and chamomile soothe her frazzled nerves and erase the day's tension from her aching shoulders.

Thoughts of the man who called himself Madd, ran rampant in her head, arousing emotions she found disturbing. The image of his muscular body was foremost in her mind. God forgive her, she wanted to rip off his clothes and ride the wild stallion until the fire in her loins was reduced to glowing embers, and then rekindle the flame and ride him again.

The dog crawled onto the sofa and rested his head in her lap, but she was not feeling very sociable. She set her half empty teacup on the coffee table and stood. She shed her clothes in a heap on the living room floor and made her way to the bathroom. She turned on the cold water and stepped into the shower. She squealed as the icy blast connected with her bare skin, but allowed the water to gush over her naked body as she scrubbed vigorously, punishing herself for her naughty thoughts of Madd.

"Damn him," she said out loud, but her inner voice

whispered things that made her heart pound and turn her cheeks a bright shade of pink.

This lewd behavior she was exhibiting was totally unacceptable. The man was turning her into a Jezebel. She wouldn't see him again, not even if he got down on his knees and begged. She giggled. She could totally foresee that not happening. She stepped out of the shower and tripped over the dog.

"You've got to stop following me into the bathroom. It's indecent."

She laughed self-consciously. She had to stop humanizing this gigantic ball of fur. He was just a poor brute looking for a little attention after being left alone for hours on end. She bent down and planted a kiss on his wet nose, slipped into her nightgown, and slid between the satin sheets. She prayed that sleep would come quickly, and it did.

The clamor of the Big Ben alarm startled her awake. As she had done a thousand times before, Angel climbed out of bed, prepared a cup of strong coffee, flipped on the television, and sat back to enjoy a few moments to herself.

The cup shattered on the floor as the top news story of the day flashed across the television screen. *Serial killer claims fourth victim*, scrolled across the screen in big bold letters, followed with the gruesome news about a mutilated body of a cabbie found beside his taxi with the motor still running.

She sat glued to the screen as the chief of police came on and said a whole lot of nothing, but reading between the lines, it appeared this corpse had been mutilated far worse than all the others. Dazed, she heard the chief yammering something about the FBI, a manhunt, and leads on the case, but she was no longer listening.

She sank to her knees as an image of the blood-spattered taxicab flashed across the screen. Number 667! Her cab! The nice driver who had brought her home only hours before had fallen victim to the madman roaming the streets like an invincible shadow. Regardless of the propaganda the chief of police was saying, she suspected that they were no closer to catching the fiend now than on the night he'd claimed his first victim.

She'd have to pay an extra fare, but if the murderer wasn't apprehended soon, she was going to take the dog with her wherever she went, even to work.

As if he'd read her thoughts, the dog whined and wagged his tail, pledging his allegiance. She dropped down beside him, wrapped her arms around his neck and wept.

"You're all I've got, dog, standing between me, Alex, and that god-awful killer. You may prove to be my salvation."

She picked up the telephone, dialed *Club Venus* and called in sick. She climbed into bed beside Alex and coaxed the dog to lie down on the foot of the bed. She stretched out a foot and tickled the dog's belly with her toes. His fur felt wet. She flipped on the bedside light. A scream formed somewhere deep inside her chest.

"Blood!"

She scrubbed her toes furiously against the sheets. Then she remembered the leftover meatloaf from the night before.

"Ketchup!" she muttered. "It's tomato ketchup."

She drifted off to sleep and dreamed of strange places, strange faces, and a yawning abyss from which there was no escape.

CHAPTER TEN

Two days off work had rested Angel's tired body, but hadn't come close to settling her frayed nerves. She had to fight against the instinct to call the club and stay locked inside her small sanctuary with the deadbolts in place for yet another day, but she knew her boss would not buy into another lame excuse.

She needed the job to pay the rent. God help those who were left to roam the streets with no place to go and a maniac on the loose! She shuddered and rousted Alex out of his warm bed. She hurriedly stripped off his pajamas and fitted him into his street clothes, ignoring his loud protests. Ordinarily, she would have let him help dress himself, but today his pleas of being a big boy fell on deaf ears.

Her hand trembled as she dialed the number of the cab company. She wouldn't be surprised if the taxi drivers refused to come to this neighborhood. It was ludicrous, but she couldn't shake the feeling she was somehow responsible for the fate of the poor man who had driven her home and fallen victim to such a horrible fate.

She paced the room. The Yellow Stripe Taxi rolling to a stop in front of the building was a beautiful sight. Taking Alex's hand, she hurried down the stairs, lifted him into the cab and climbed in beside him. She gripped the edge of her seat and remained silent as the driver steered through the streets, disregarding traffic signals, swerving around pedestrians at crosswalks, and cutting off traffic as though the hounds of hell were on his tail. She breathed a sigh of relief when she dropped Alex with the sitter. She climbed back into the taxi, sat on the edge of her seat, and prayed the brakes were in good working order.

When the cab slid to a stop in front of the club, she bolted from the vehicle and slammed the door hard. Guilt forced her to tip more than she could afford. Now, she'd have to work extra hours and arrive home later than usual, putting her and Alex at an even greater risk.

She laughed. The harsh sound vibrated eerily in her throat. The lateness of the hour wouldn't make any difference one way or another. Nobody wanted to get involved. Someone was always arguing or slugging it out within the paper-thin walls of the apartments. The pimps knocked around the street girls, and gang members ran rampant, terrorizing anyone brave enough to venture onto the streets. Screams in her neighborhood were not an unusual occurrence. Even the police turned a deaf ear and a blind eye unless the crime was so heinous it was picked up by the media.

She hurried inside the club. She stashed her purse and pretended not to notice the on-duty hatcheck girl's red face and unpretentious angry glances at the clock. So what if she was a few minutes late. A few extra minutes wouldn't kill the girl.

Angel stopped short. *Bad choice of words.* Murder was the last thing she wanted to think about right now. She called out a 'sorry' at the girl's departing back, but her words were cut off by the slamming door. The snippy little twit could piss off and die for all she cared. Angel McKeough had bigger fish to fry.

****

She could feel eyes watching her, and this time, she knew exactly who it was…Madd! He was somewhere in the confines of the club. The man was stuck in her head. Where he was concerned, her senses were fine-tuned with the precision of a bat's sonar system. She patted her hair and powdered her nose from her makeup compact. She watched the clock and mechanically performed her job as she waited for him to appear.

A half hour passed, and then an hour, and he had not made his presence known. *Well!* Angel McKeough would not wait around to pick up leftovers when the club's whores had finished with Mr. Madd.

She smiled charmingly at the men passing by, exchanging pleasantries, pretending to be flattered by the comments bestowed on her, not saying yes, but not saying no to propositions of a more suggestive nature.

The hair stood on the back of her neck as she caught a glimpse of Madd elbowing his way through the line of eager Casanovas vying for her attention. She leaned on the counter, revealing lots of cleavage, and grinned at a slightly heavyset man as Madd shouldered his way to the head of the line.

Moses parting the Red Sea. She laughed. "Where are you going in such a hurry, honey?"

"Hello, Angel girl."

A cold shiver went up her spine. His words were soft as the Chinchilla fur she'd just checked, but a storm raged in those amber eyes.

She ignored his angry scowl and gave him a saucy grin. She allowed her fingers to brush his and linger a brief second as she took the check ticket from his hand. Red flags popped in her mind. She had already strayed off the familiar path and was venturing deep into the wild side. Something inside her snapped and pushed her to the brink of madness. She might just have met the big, bad wolf, but he didn't frighten her one little bit.

She laughed at the complicity of it all. Her pulse fluttered as she watched the muscles chord in his jaw. His voice was harsh and cold.

"My coat!"

"Hold on, sweetie. There's just one little ol' me and a whole bunch of you fine gentlemen." She fluttered her lashes. "No need to push and shove. I'll get around to the lot of you in due time."

She giggled. She eyed him cautiously and waited for his reaction to her bold remark. She pouted her lips, her tongue tracing the outline of their fullness. The wet sheen glistened on the bright red lipstick, tantalizing and inviting.

She stood her ground as he pushed his body halfway across the counter, bringing his face within inches of her own. The pools of rich amber in his eyes had turned to molten lava. She could see his mouth moving, but his words were lost in the savage pounding of her heart and the roar of excitement among the patrons. Something inside her screamed danger! She liked the way it made her feel.

She leaned forward, closing the gap between Madd and her. She cupped his face between her hands and pressed her lips to his. She meant to humiliate him, arouse his animalistic desires and leave him hard and dry, but she was disappointed to find his body remained rigid and unresponsive. Two red spots stained her cheeks. She had misread the guy. This jerk didn't give a damn about her! She'd merely been a distraction, a pawn in an evening of fun and games. She took his bottom lip between her teeth and bit down hard.

"First blood," she whispered against his cheek.

She had a sinking feeling she'd just opened Pandora's Box, even though he left without saying a word.

She felt sick. She pushed a stack of coats across the counter for the gentlemen to sort out and made a hasty retreat to the women's facility. *Good God! What had she gotten herself into?*

The face staring back from the mirror was pale and haggard. No amount of cold water splashed on her fevered cheeks could extinguish the fire burning out of control deep within her soul.

She was glad her shift was coming to an end. For once, she was happy at the prospect of going home to her little apartment. She wanted to seal herself away from the cruel world and the man who called himself, Madd.

She was a stark raving lunatic! She'd behaved scandalously and launched an assault against one of the patrons of the club. She prayed the man didn't make a complaint against her.

She implored the club bouncer to walk her outside to the taxicab, thankful he didn't ask questions. Her eyes searched the darkness, expecting Madd to spring out of the shadows to seek revenge on the harlot who had dared to challenge his manliness.

When she thought about it, that's exactly what she'd done, thrown down the gauntlet and declared war. She recalled the barbaric thrill at the taste of his blood on her lips. He hadn't even flinched. He wouldn't let her blatant assault pass, she was certain of it. There was only one thing she could do—run.

As the irony of the situation hit home, she put her head in her hands and sighed heavily. She was caught in an impossible situation. The thought of never seeing Madd again was more than she could bear. She was head over heels in love with an insensitive bastard that was only out for cheap thrills.

"No! It can't be love."

She had just met the man and engaged in inconsequential polite conversation over a cup of coffee. She was in lust. That's what it was. Those sensual nightmares of hers must have awakened some dormant mutant sex gene.

She had been a wild thing, charging the man like a bull elephant in musk. And Madd…he had stood there, his lips clamped tightly together so cold, she wondered why her lips hadn't stuck to his like the time she had stuck her tongue against a metal pole on a cold winter's morning. It had been a stupid thing to do, but she had to put the humiliation behind her. She would put this audacious incident behind her, too. She cringed in the corner of the taxicab and tried not to think about it.

What's done is done, she told herself.

It would be a cold day in hell before she'd admit she had feelings for that whoremonger. If he wanted to take up the gauntlet, so be it. Let him think what he chose to think. This was one working girl with a few tricks of her own up her sleeve.

She laughed loudly at her choice of words, causing the cabbie to squirm nervously in his seat and bump the curb as he pulled in front of her building. She was glad the ride was over. Judging from the way the driver snatched the money from her hand and departed before the door slammed shut, he was even more relieved than her.

Her steps dragged as she climbed the stairs. Alex was dead weight across her shoulder. She prayed he wouldn't wake when she put him in bed. She needed time to think.

She'd apologize should she ever see Madd again, but she'd not grovel before him like a dog sniveling in the presence of a beast master.

"Ah, shit!"

She'd forgotten the dog again. She called to him, but he was nowhere to be found. In her haste, she must've forgotten to let him back inside before she left for work. It was wrong to turn him loose on his own, but she had no choice. So far, he'd always found his way home.

She was bone tired. She dropped her clothes beside the bed and crawled under the covers. The satin sheets were cool against her bare skin, making her shiver. She hugged the pillow against her body and thought of Madd. She couldn't decide if his return would be a good or bad thing. The question reverberated in her head like ninepins until she drifted off to sleep. Then the dreams started.

She lay perfectly still in the darkness. Logic told her she was alone, but she sensed a presence. She held her breath. In the stillness, the sound of breathing was clearly audible. She pinched herself.

"Ouch!" That hurt. The pain seemed real enough.

"I am here, my lovely."

"Oh, my God!" she whispered. These lucid romantic rendezvous were robbing her of her sanity. Fantasy and reality were all jumbled in her head. The whispering voice in her ear was vaguely disturbing. She knew that voice, just couldn't remember from where. The answer was irrelevant. Her dream lover was nothing more than a configuration conjured from the dark recesses of a sexually deprived body and a sleep deprived brain.

The sensations her body was experiencing were certainly no figment of her imagination. The pulsating fiery passion building between her legs felt as though her pussy was going to explode.

The bulb of his cock tantalized her wetness. She opened her legs and pressed her body against his, trying to initiate penetration. This was her lucid dream and, this time, the dream would not end before her body found release.

"Fuck me! Dammit. Fuck me!"

His lips trailed down her face, lingered on her neck for a tantalizing few seconds, then nibbled her nipples.

"Ask for it. Beg, bitch."

She moaned softly as he flipped her on her back and dropped on top of her.

"Fuck me," she said again, her voice thick with desire.

He obliged, thrusting hard and burrowing deep. Pain and ecstasy collided with blunt force. She raked her nails across his back and prayed he hadn't split her all the way back to her asshole.

She begged him to stop; then begged him to fuck her harder. She arched her back, taking all he had to give. Her legs wrapped around his waist and drew him still deeper inside her. She cried out as his hands circled her buttocks in a firm grasp, lifting her body to mold against his as he exploded, filling her.

"Yes! Yes! Yesssssss!" A thousand torches combusted inside her vagina, curling her toes. She trembled as cold shivers tingled her body, fire and ice, contracting and expanding until she thought she would die of sheer ecstasy.

He stayed inside her until the rapturous contractions had subsided, leaving her exhausted. She felt him slip away and roll off her. Her hand fumbled for the lamp switch, then fell limp back on the bed. Why bother? She would wake and he would be gone. She sighed heavily. If she didn't know better, she would swear she could feel the pressure of a body lying on the opposite side of the bed. She stretched out her hand. Emptiness.

Holy shit! It *was* only a dream! The remnants of a sleep induced trance, but what a dream! She'd thought men were the only ones who had wet dreams. This was better than the real thing.

She felt a stab of shame as Charlie's picture grinned at her from the bedside table. She lifted it to her mouth and kissed his cold lips. Pangs of guilt tinged her consciousness but didn't squelch the splendor of the moment.

"Sorry, honey."

She laid the photo face down, closed her eyes and slept like a baby.

CHAPTER ELEVEN

Garmin stood staring down at the sleeping figure lying on the bed. Angel looked like the picture of innocence, but the bitch was a black widow. She had set the trap and he'd taken the bait, snared like a fly in her web of lust. He took a step back from the bed, resisting the urge to run the tip of his finger along the contours of her voluptuous breasts and tweak the erect nipples, still pink from his passionate kisses.

He'd fine-tuned her like a Stradivarius, but he was the one who had been played. He'd underestimated her level of cunning. He had fallen victim to her womanly wiles, allowing her to breach his safety zone and get inside his head.

He blew an audible breath. He had come close to blowing his cover tonight. He'd been mounting bitches for hundreds of years, but he had never experienced such fire in his loins as had transpired this night. He wanted to go back and do it all again, with the lights on. He dabbed sweat off his forehead, but his skin felt clammy. Were his balls turning into marshmallows?

"Nah!"

What he experienced had been nothing more than a testosterone rush triggered by the cumulative effects of pent-up desires. He could deal with lust. Lust was a natural urge that could be quenched in a single act, but once *love* latched its barbed tentacles around the heart, it chipped away the hard crust and molded the soft center to its own liking. Garmin Maximilian was too proud and too crafty to succumb to an affliction that robbed one of free will. Love. Even the word left a vile taste in his mouth.

He did feel a sense of pride. The woman and he made a good pair; but she was proud and strong willed, two undesirable traits, but he'd bring her around. Bitches were meant to serve their mate without question, putting his needs before anything else. As second in command to The Dark Mother, his bitch would carry some clout. The way she conducted herself would set an exemplary standard throughout the realms of the Kingdom of the Dead.

The issue of the boy was an unanticipated stumbling block, to which he hoped to find a painless solution. In the natural order of things, females separated from their young with no ill effects, but human bitches seemed to draw it out a lot longer than nature intended. The issue was not up for debate. His word was law, but the return journey would be less strenuous if Angel was a willing traveler.

He knew she had strong feelings toward him. He'd felt her tremble with desire when she kissed him at the club. Eternity would not be long enough with such a woman.

He was ready to look her square in the face, reveal his true identity, confess his…declare his intentions, and return home with his bride. He was done with hiding in the shadows of her dreams.

The tangled web of deceit he had spun in order to make first contact bound his feet and stifled his tongue. He, a mighty warrior that answered to nobody, was stuck in this wretched concrete jungle, living a dog's life existence, when he could be in the halls of Hel's Castle living like a king. His dignity would not suffer the abomination for much longer. The situation had to be remedied soon before he began to lift his leg to take a piss.

He'd pursue the present ruse a little longer while he contemplated the separation of mother and child. The boy had been a thorn in his hide from the get-go. He'd had just about enough of those big, round, innocent eyes prying into his business, whining and tattling to his mommy about *The Man*. Maybe, he should show the little snitch just what he was up against.

He had been careful to shapeshift away from the inquisitive eyes of the boy, but somehow, the obstinate little turd could see through his illusions. The boy's description of *The Man* was becoming more graphic and more detailed with each daily revelation.

So far, Angel had dismissed the boy's night terrors as anxiety stemming from something he may have seen or overheard about the crazed maniac on the loose. But the seed of suspicion had been planted. Angel was beginning to ask questions and search for answers. Sooner or later, she would hit upon the truth, and he didn't want the excitement of his coming disclosure to be warped by the boy's premature ramblings.

He was proud of his species. He would tell Angel. He needed to gain her trust...prepare her so her brain wouldn't short circuit when he granted her the privilege of viewing his magnificent Kanimorph presence.

Perhaps he needed to try a little friendly persuasion to entice the boy to keep his jaws shut, or better still, cut to the chase and erase the brat's birth certificate, eliminating all traces of his existence. Might as well do the dirty deed right! A dry chuckle prickled the inner lining of his throat, but his laughter held no mirth. Something was jabbing at him, annoying little tweaks disrupting his state of consciousness.

"Time shift," he mumbled.

He padded softly into the room and stared down at the sleeping child. His canines dropped and his lips pulled back in a snarl. Saliva dribbled onto the child's face. He pulled back as the boy mumbled, "Mommy" and stretched out his thin little arms.

He felt a sudden urge to pick the boy up and comfort him as he'd seen Angel do many times. Beads of sweat popped out on his forehead. His temples were beginning to throb. What *was* he thinking? Garmin Maximilian neither showed mercy nor took prisoners. His course of action was clear.

He trailed his finger down the pale cheek of the sleeping child, his razor sharp nail drawing blood. The boy whimpered and flipped over on his back, still entranced in sleep. Garmin hovered above him.

"Alex," he whispered, but the boy didn't stir. He flipped on the bedside light and stood ready to silence the boy's cries. He watched as the child rubbed his eyes and shielded his face from the light.

"Alex," he repeated, louder this time. He grunted with satisfaction when the boy's eyes widened in recognition.

"Oh, it's you," Alex mumbled sleepily. "Why man wearing ugly skin? Alex likes man skin best."

"Ah! You think the man's ugly, do you?"

The boy's lips puckered. "I want my Mommy."

"Don't worry about Mommy," Garmin said mockingly. He leaned over Alex and placed a sharp claw underneath the child's quivering chin. "You'd best be worried about Alex—"

His words were cut short as the boy shoved the offending digit aside, leaving a long red whelp on his skin. The child rose to his knees and clinched his small fists. "Man hurt Mommy; Alex hurt man."

Garmin stepped back, visibly shaken. Dormant memories surged to the surface of his consciousness, taking him by surprise. There was a time long ago when he'd fought hard against insurmountable odds to protect his mother, a battle he'd lost. His eyes softened as he recalled the gentle maiden who'd fought like a warrior the day he had been snatched from her arms. She, too, had lost the battle.

Hands…lots of hands…had carried him in one direction and his mother in another. He hadn't seen her since that fateful day.

The experience had made him stronger. He'd sworn on that dark day he'd never again open his heart to hurt, and he had not. He took what he wanted and destroyed anything that stood in his way. He had no conscience and felt no remorse for his actions. It was a matter of pride and principle rolled into one burning desire to inflict pain and suffering as he had been made to suffer, to render justice for deeds unpunished. As a baby, he had been weak and dependent on his mother. He had been taken from her and cast into a world where only the strong survived. He had survived. His lip curled. *Conquer and destroy, get them before they get you.*

In honor of his mother, he'd spare the boy. He might consider taking him on the return journey as long as he was put into service far away in a distant realm of the kingdom. Perhaps he'd allow Alex to visit his mommy every two or three hundred years, if the young pup kept his nose out of *The Man's* affairs.

He leaned close and whispered into the boy's ear. A satisfied grin spread across his face as the child dove underneath the covers and lay still.

Garmin stared into nothingness, his eyes blanketed in thought. Death had no jurisdiction over those gifted with immortality in The Dark Mother's kingdom. He uttered a dry mirthless chuckle. Immortality in the land of the dead, how ironic.

He folded his canines, drew his claws in and shapeshifted back into human form. In time, he would teach Angel how to shapeshift. Then, she could change her form into a presence pleasing to him, matching his own natural stately appearance, much the same as his personification of the human form found favor in her eyes.

Leaving the boy in the picture might not prove to be such a bad thing. As a matter of fact, it could be the factor that turned the tide in his favor. Let the little snip talk until he was blue in the face about *The Man*. It would only convince his mommy he needed a father figure in his life. A throaty growl rumbled in his throat and slipped past his lips in a chorus of robust laughter. He watched the lump underneath the cover rise and fall in a steady rhythm and a frown puckered his brow.

"Hmm!"

This was not part of the master plan. Perhaps he should renege on his decision to spare the boy. He took a step toward the bed and leaned heavily against the bedpost. A large knot formed in the center of his chest, sending waves of nausea breaking against the pit of his gut. Perspiration beaded his forehead. The mere thought of harming the child made him want to vomit. He backed hastily out of the room and bolted for the front door.

He hesitated, turned and veered toward Angel's bedroom. He watched her as she slept. He hadn't noticed the tiny brown mole near the corner of her mouth, but he found it most appealing. He was tempted to strip off the sheet and see what other secrets lurked in the contours of that luscious body, but he suspected the boy was playing possum until the coast was clear. At any minute, the child was likely to come running into the room, all wide eyed, with yet another tale about *The Man*.

He smoothed the damp silky strands of hair back from Angel's face and pulled the sheet a little higher up on her chest, then exited the room and slipped through the front door. His enthusiasm for the hide-and-seek stratagem was waning. Soon, he'd show himself and make his move. Soon!

The night lights turned his prominent features into fuzzy shadows as he stepped into the street. It matched his state of mind. His brain was confused, hazed by all the turmoil raging in his soul, if he had such a thing. He could make whatever lame excuse he pleased, but the truth of the matter was plain and simple: he didn't want to destroy the boy. He admired the little pup's spunk. With proper training, the boy would be a great warrior whom he'd be proud to call son.

He definitely had nothing to lose by accepting a package deal. If the pair posed too many complications, he could always turn the boy over to The Dark Mother, but the action would undoubtedly lose favor with the woman.

"Dammit!" He didn't need to gain favor with his bitch. He was the Big Dog Daddy, not some pussy whipped puppy.

"Trivial matters," he muttered.

He had a more pressing situation to think about. His time in this world was set to expire in a few days, and he'd not begun to prepare for the return trip. Since he was contemplating taking on yet another new charge, the journey would be rough and reentry most unpleasant.

The Maiden would have figured out his treachery and would not be in an accommodating frame of mind. Maybe the old battle-axe would relent if he told her he'd been pining for *her* all the time he was gone. He chuckled. The Maiden wouldn't fall for that line and frankly, trying to bone that withered pussy would be like boring a hole into an ironwood tree with his dick.

He shrugged. He'd gotten out and he'd get back in, even if he had to tear The Maiden limb from limb.

"Que sera, sera."

****

The urge came suddenly, a burning desire for one last hunt. He'd found very little satisfaction hunting down these human simpletons. His eyes iced over and his lips thinned. Why not sharpen the odds with multiple opponents?

He patrolled the streets. He paid no heed to groups of figures huddled in dark allies passing around strange smoking sticks, or the scantily clad whores that accosted the motor cars moving along the streets. All were easy pickings, but not what he needed tonight.

A faded tin sign caught his eye. It dangled hapha-zardly on a broken chain, marking the entrance to a hole in the wall. Even in poor lighting, he could see the sign was riddled with bullet holes. A big grin curved his lips as he read the lettering.

He walked into the *Devil's Den*, ripped off his hat and tossed it onto the middle of the floor. He stood with hands on hips and legs apart. His eyes combed the dimly lit room.

"I dare any of you sons-of-bitches to step on it."

The walls seemingly came alive as a score of burly figures, waving knives, cue sticks, and heavy chains, took up the challenge. He dodged their advances and retreated out the door, hugging the shadows. A satisfied grin split his face as the barflies followed blindly, brandishing their weapons and uttering death threats. When the light from the tall poles petered out, he turned to face his attackers.

"Bring it on, boys. This is going to hurt you more than it does me."

Garmin offered no resistance as the gang rushed him, allowing his opponents the right to first blood.

The sweet tang of fresh blood stimulated the olfacto-ry regions of the brain. A piercing battle cry rent the air as he ripped the heads off the three closest adversaries and hurled them at the retreating backs of the pack. He swiftly overtook his antagonists. Within minutes the bar-flies lay scattered at his feet and his howl of victory shat-tered the eerie silence encompassing the chaos of a few moments earlier.

He was sorely disappointed. One or many had not made any notable difference. A whole gang of mortals could not come close to matching the prowess of a single dark warrior. To give the devil his due, he had cheated a bit. He chuckled and coaxed the inner beast into submission.

He took his time, drinking freely of the salty nectar and gorging on the still warm flesh. He plucked the hearts from the heartiest specimens and devoured them in rending gulps. The essence hit him with the force of a lightning bolt, literally bringing him to his knees. This was a bastardly bunch of street vermin. He'd never felt so empowered, and he loved it!

He cast off his garments and proceeded to lick his wounds and cleanse his body. He was pleasantly surprised to see the gang had gotten in several good blows. This group was worthy of memorializing after all. He aligned the like pieces in a perfect circle, with a pyramid of heads in the center.

As he stood admiring his mortal shrine, it suddenly dawned on him that in his blood lust, he'd overlooked one small detail, a change of clothing!

It would surely have the blue boys blowing their horns if he was seen in his blood-drenched clothing. He was left with one option. He paraded naked down the street swinging low and free, drawing gasps of awe from passersby and jamming traffic as motorists' headlamps spotlighted his beastly genitalia.

Dawn was streaking the morning sky before he found a suitable score, but he had hit it big. The man had a case full of clothes and a stuffed wallet. At last, Garmin had the means to treat his lady to the best cuisine this miserable city had to offer, and travel in style for the remainder of his stay. His step was light as he headed toward Angel's home.

Without warning, the exhilaration from the simultaneous absorption of seven mean bastards' essence flip-flopped into a raging hatred that gang raped his mind. A faint ray of reasoning penetrated the dark recesses of his turmoil. It wasn't safe to return to the woman in this state of mind, and he certainly wasn't in the mood to transform into the docile, obedient character he portrayed. As a matter of fact, plan A had run its course.

No more dicking around. He was stepping up his game. He'd turn on the charm, shower Angel with flowers and chocolates, and be so nice to sweet little Alex, the child would call him daddy.

"Wine 'em, dine 'em, fuck 'em, take 'em home and introduce 'em to Mother."

It was a sobering thought. He *would* have to introduce Angel to The Dark Mother on his return, and he wasn't looking forward to the aftermath that was sure to follow. The Dark Mother would not be pleased to see history repeating itself. Like father like son meant another shattered fanatical delusion for The Dark Mother. But now was not the time to think about stirring the honey pot and resurrecting the green-eyed monster.

His strategy was mapped out. He had two whole days to woo Angel. On the third day, he'd lay his cards on the table and see if the lady played or folded. Either way, he was returning to his world and taking her with him.

As long as the child kept his mouth shut, his plans should go off without a hitch.

He smiled and repeated a phrase from earlier in the evening.

Lucid Dreams

"Que sera, sera."

CHAPTER TWELVE

Angel was awakened by shrill screams coming from the vicinity of Alex's room. She bounded out of her bedroom, grabbed a robe off the old paint-spattered wooden chair and ran into Alex's room. She thought it strange that the light was on. The sight of her baby drawn into a ball, clutching the covers around his head and babbling incoherently about *The Man* pushed the question from her mind.

She gathered Alex close to her bosom. The tremors racking his tiny body were so strong, her arms vibrated.

"Man going to eat Alex," he sobbed.

"Shhh. Mommy won't let anything hurt you, sweetheart."

She rocked him back and forth, pushing his hair back and planting gentle kisses on his forehead. He was wringing wet with perspiration, and his eyes, black with fear, appeared too large for his face. She held him and sang softly until his head dropped onto her chest and his body relaxed. These nightmares were becoming more frequent and were always about *The Man*. Where in the hell did this figure who invaded her child's dreams come from?

Looking back, she realized Alex's nightmares had started about the same time as the street murders. In the beginning, she'd thought maybe he'd heard something on television, but it had to be darker, more complex...and sinister.

She placed Alex back on his pillow and lay down beside him, cradling him in her arms. Come to think of it, her erotic dreams had also started at the same time as

Alex's nightmares. If his dreams were remotely close to the realism she'd experienced, it was no wonder the poor little guy was scared half to death.

Something was going on that she didn't understand. It was insane to surmise some phantom intruder stole into her bedroom in the wee hours of the night to ravish her body, traumatize her son, and then disappear before morning light. But her dreams were more than a glitch in reality. She'd reached heights and sensations beyond anything she'd experienced…beyond anything she'd thought her body capable of feeling. Her dream lover had coaxed her into contorting her body to seemingly impossible positions that maximized pleasure and had her screaming and clawing like a jungle cat.

She shamefully acknowledged she looked forward to falling asleep each night with as much anticipation and awe as a virgin bride on her wedding night.

She'd said things and done things during these lucid love sessions that even in the sanctity of the marriage bed would've been disturbing.

As real as the late night love sessions seemed, she needed a genuine man. She wanted someone who would be there when she opened her eyes in the morning. Perhaps if he was still interested, she would be more receptive to the charming Mr. Madd, although she'd insist on knowing his real name before she wedded and bedded him. She was an old fashioned girl and the two intertwined, although in this modern day and age, not necessarily in that order.

She laughed at her own impudence. It was highly unlikely that Madd would ever want to see her again. A man like that could have all the action he craved from the working girls at the club and, yet, he'd shunned their advances for a cup of coffee and a bit of conservation with a prudish hat check girl.

Madd must've seen something he liked about her. If he showed up at the club again, she'd apologize for her outrageous behavior and ask *him* out for a cup of coffee. If nothing else, her job at the club had educated her on the sexual revolution that had taken the country by storm.

She'd been out of the dating game for a while, but she still remembered the ritual. Today's meat market was more about lust than love, but she refused to accept anything less than a healthy combination of both.

She stood in front of the shabby old dresser, staring at her reflection. She ran her hands over her body. Her breasts were her most prominent asset, voluptuous and pointed. In spite of their size, these babies had done a damn good job of defying gravity.

Their size had always been a source of embarrassment, drawing admiring glances from husbands and lovers who would have gladly paid good money to purchase a duplicate pair for their lady, if it was possible to do so. On the flip side, there were the disdainful looks from sweethearts and wives who would've liked nothing better than to see the pair deflate and sag precariously down her chest. She smiled at the thought. She hated to disappoint, but her breasts were a natural enhancement.

She twisted and turned trying to get a better view of her buttocks. The cheeks were round and firm. Not too bad for an old woman of twenty-seven!

She laughed at her foolishness, feeling excited and alive for the first time in a long while. God had blessed her with a healthy set of knockers and well-padded bottom. She was through apologizing. She'd put her rounded figure up against the skinny bitches at the club any day.

She flung open the closet door and flipped through the neat row of racked dresses she'd abandoned since Charlie's passing. She selected a sassy little silver colored mini cut halfway to the waist. She slipped it over her head, pleased to see it molded her body perfectly. She giggled. Angel McKeough was back in the game, hot to trot and on the prowl. Madd didn't know it yet, but he was a had lad.

She arrived to work ahead of schedule, dressed for success. She found a seat inside the club, facing the door. She sat alone, sipping on a virgin pina colada. No more strong liquor would pass through her lips.

She waited, rehearsing in her mind the *'I'm sorry'* spiel she planned to drop on Madd. She jumped and stifled a scream when a familiar voice whispered into her ear.

"Waiting for someone?"

Madd's eyes told her exactly what she had hoped to hear, boosting her courage.

"Yes." She blinked her lashes and wet her lips. A blush stole over her cheeks. "You."

A delightful tingling sensation traveled through her body and exited out her toes as he slid his chair close and lifted her hand to his lips.

"I've been waiting for you, too, Angel girl."

Her breathing quickened and her heart soared as the warmth of his breath caressed her knuckles.

Unbridled passion kindled his eyes. "Shall we start over? I'm not Madd." He laughed. "Well, some might think so, but my real name is Garmin Maximilian. May I ask what an Angel is doing in this den of sinners?"

She smiled across the table. "That's a terrible pick-up line." She dropped her eyes. "At the risk of sounding redundant, my answer to your question is, I'm waiting for you." She glanced at him through her lashes, mustering her courage. "I wanted to apologize for the green monster that reared its ugly head the last time we met. I, too, was hoping we could start over." She leaned in close. "May I buy you a cup of coffee after I finish my shift, Garmin?"

"I was thinking along those lines, but how about I buy, and right now?" he asked.

"Oh, no, I really can't afford to—"

"Forgive me for being presumptuous, but I've asked for your hand, so to speak, and the manager has graciously given you the night off."

Her jaw dropped in total disbelief as he stood and pushed her chair away from the table, offering his arm.

"Shall we go?"

She allowed him to escort her out the door. A long black limousine waited with the driver standing ready. She stopped. "What's this?" The way Garmin was smiling down at her made her heart skip a beat. She didn't resist when he urged her forward.

"I thought something a little classier than the all-night diner would be more appropriate for a new beginning," he said smoothly.

She stepped inside the car and was overwhelmed with a mixture of excitement and dread as he slid in beside her. He gave instructions to the driver and closed off the outside world. He seemed to sense her apprehension and quickly poured two glasses of sparkling bubbly, handing her a glass.

"Good wine, good time. Is it not the custom in your world?"

She laughed. "It's a nice custom in any world. Pray tell, what world do you come from?" The serious expression on his face troubled her, as did his words.

He slid across the seat. His thigh pressed lightly against hers.

"All in good time."

The breath caught in Angel's throat. She had heard those words spoken before. *Thank God he couldn't read her thoughts.* A blush stole over her cheeks as she recalled vividly the circumstances leading up to that prior statement.

Garmin cocked an eyebrow. "Am I responsible for the delightful color on your cheeks?"

"Hardly," she muttered.

She swallowed a huge gulp of wine, choking off her oxygen. She didn't protest when Garmin took the glass from her hand and gently touched his lips to hers, then passionately, his tongue begging her lips to open and accept him.

She closed her eyes and molded her body against his. Reveling in the flames of passion, she surrendered completely.

'Enjoy the moment, girl', her heart whispered, but her brain screamed, *'Stop!'*

She didn't listen to either. Madd's kisses tasted too good to stop, and she didn't want to merely enjoy the moment, she was committed to the whole show. She begged him to take her there in the limousine, but he disengaged himself from her embrace and moved away.

"Not yet, my Angel. I want you to get to know the real me."

"My thoughts exactly," she whispered, and reached for him. She pulled his head down, taking possession of his mouth, but he drew back.

She saw a glimmer of excitement flicker in his eyes as he leaned toward her.

"I guess you could say I have a secret. Once it's out of the way, neither hell nor heaven can keep you from me."

She willingly accepted the glass of wine Garmin handed her, then another and another. She pouted her lips.

"What's this big secret you need to get off your chest?" She winked and lay back on the seat, purring like a kitten. "Something off your chest, something on mine." She placed his hands on her breasts. "I like my idea better."

Garmin pulled his hands from her grasp.

"What I have to say needs to be said in private, just between you and me. Would you consent to stopping off at my humble abode if I promise to be a true gentleman?"

Angel giggled. "Only if you promise you won't!"

She held out her wine glass to be refilled, but he took it from her fingers just as the car pulled up to the luxurious Plaza Hotel.

"What you need is hot coffee, strong and bitter."

She followed him into a suite apartment and sat on a wraparound sofa among a heaped pile of cushions. She sighed with contentment as he placed more pillows behind her back and lifted her feet to rest on an ottoman softer than the pillows.

The plush surroundings brought back recollections of happier times, along with painful memories she'd fought hard to suppress. She'd been accustomed to accommodations like this when Charlie was alive. But she wasn't going to think of Charlie right now. He would always hold a special place in her heart, but she had to let go, start over and learn to live again.

She smiled at Garmin hovering above her, appreciating his efforts to please her, even though it made him seem like a doting idiot. She instinctively knew this wasn't the case. She found it hard to believe this man had ever doted in his life, and he certainly was no idiot.

She patted the sofa beside her, shuffling the cushions to make way for him to sit next to her, but he dropped to one knee instead. He took her hand and slipped a diamond on her finger. It fit perfectly. The brilliance of the marble-sized stone left her gasping for breath.

She pinched herself to see if she was awake or dreaming. Garmin held her hand captive, kissing her fingertips one after the other; then turning her hand to place his lips against her palm.

"I apologize for the size of the stone. Such beauty and delicacy should not be overshadowed by an ornament."

"Ornament!" she whispered hoarsely. "This is the most gorgeous ring I've ever seen, but what's the meaning of this? We barely know each other. I have a child."

She forgot to breathe as he took her face between his hands and looked into her eyes.

"You are my chosen one," he said. "I knew it the

first time I saw you." He looked deeply into her eyes and smiled. "The fact that I'll gain a son in the process is, how you say, more icing on the cake."

She gasped. This was insane, straight from the pages of a Grimm's fairy tale. But Garmin was handsome and seemed so humble, kneeling at her feet as if she was a queen! The wine must've sizzled her brain because she was halfway considering taking him up on his offer.

She stretched out her arms invitingly. "Shouldn't we at least try it out to see if it fits before taking the final step?"

She giggled at his stunned expression.

"That's the nectar of the grapes talking," he said and disappeared into the kitchen. He was back in a matter of seconds with a steaming cup of black coffee.

"Drink. We need to talk."

"Do tell," she replied, taking a gulp of the scalding liquid. She sprayed it out her mouth, panting to cool her scorched tongue.

Garmin dabbed at the brown stain spreading across the front of her dress, but she puckered her lips and tried to pull him down on the seat beside her.

"I'm hot...and wet."

She arrogantly extended her pinkie and took a small sip of coffee. She winked and slicked her tongue across her lips. "Want some?" She giggled. "I don't mean coffee, honey."

She reluctantly allowed him to wrestle the cup from her hand. She drew a quick breath, causing her to bite her tongue as he slammed the cup down hard against the table. She saw his teeth clench.

"Are you sober enough to understand the importance of what I'm about to tell you?"

She sighed heavily. "Yup."

She wished he would shut up. Conversation wasn't exactly what she had in mind. Did this man have ice water in his testicles? She'd done everything short of raping him, and he wanted to talk!

****

Garmin sat down beside Angel and took both her hands. "I'm from a place far away…a different realm, and I must return shortly. Come with me and I'll give you anything your heart desires."

He twisted the diamond ring around her finger. "This rock you find so fascinating is nothing compared to the treasures waiting at the end of our journey. You and your boy will want for naught for tens of thousands of years, forever. What I'm offering is immortality."

He could almost hear the wheels turning in her head as her face clouded with confusion.

"Yes, my Angel, you and I shall be together for all eternity. You will be as beautiful in a thousand years as you are at this very moment."

"What about my son?" she whispered. He could see the confusion on her face as she struggled to comprehend what he told her.

"The boy, too, will be immortal. What greater blessing could a mother bestow upon her child?"

He felt a sharp tug on his hands as she tried to break free of his grasp.

"I've gotta go," she whispered. "It's time to pick up Alex—"

He held her hands tighter. "Time doesn't matter in the land of the…in my homeland. There's only forever."

He watched the color drain from Angel's face and her fingers fumble for the small gold cross hanging round her neck.

"No!" he said. "I'm not one of those blood sucker creatures of the night. I promise your transition will be quite painless."

He loosened his grip and she pulled her hands free.

"Let me sleep on it," she stuttered, edging toward the door. "I'm much too tired to make a decision of such magnitude tonight. I really should go."

He took her elbow and guided her back to the sofa. "The best is yet to come." He smiled. "There's one more little detail, but I'll have to show you this one."

He stood in front of her. Excitement lit his face a rosy red and his eyes twinkled like a clear, night sky.

"Close your eyes and promise not to peek." He watched Angel's eyes squeeze tightly together, her face pucker, and her fingers clench into fists. "Good!" He had her undivided attention.

He shapeshifted into his primal Kanimorph form. Wait until the woman got a load of his magnificent presence, a perfect blending of man and beast!

"Olly olly oxen free." He opened his arms wide. "Both eyes open!"

He held his breath in anticipation as she opened first one eye, and then the other. His smile faded as her eyes grew round and her mouth opened in a blood-curdling scream.

He shifted back into man form and caught her arm as she struggled to her feet and bolted toward the door.

What was wrong with the neurotic little bitch? He didn't have the time or the patience for the hard to get game. His lips thinned and a muscle twitched in his jaw.

"We leave tonight. Go gather your child and whatever small trinkets you want to carry with you. No burdensome items, please. We have a long way to go and must travel light. Everything you need will be provided for you when we arrive at our destination."

He ignored her feeble attempts to break free of his grip. His Angel girl had spirit. He found that pleasing, but the woman would do as she was told.

"We must hurry. The boy will slow us down considerably. The shadow of darkness will provide safe passage, and already the air grows pale."

"Leave my son out of it," Angel said, kicking his shins. "You touch Alex and I'll take you apart no matter how big and ugly you are."

His face went blank. "Yes, my Angel."

He watched red streaks stain her pale cheeks. The bitch was even more beautiful when she was angry!

He gasped in disbelief as she snatched the ring from her finger and flung it at his face.

"Go back to whatever demon spawned you and leave my world, my son, and me, alone!"

His arm shot out and caught the ring midair. The nerve of the bitch! Anger torched his face. He grasped her shoulders. His fingers dug into her flesh.

"I make no apologies for who or what I am," he said, his voice harsh and cold. "This world you find so appealing put me in a cage and whittled away at me like a lab rat. A babe in arms snatched from its mother because it didn't fit into the mold of what was perceived as *normal*.

My mother fled, taking me with her to the land of my father. I can only assume she fared no better in his world than I did in this one, because I was taken away and never saw her again."

He loosened his grip slightly, surprised that Angel did not try to run away. Her eyes were two huge black polka dots on a blank white canvas. He watched her through narrowed eyelids. The way her body trembled, he feared the woman was going to break into pieces.

A smile shadowed his lips, but a thin sheet of black ice glazed his eyes. He stretched out his hand and she took it. The mist in her eyes began to spill over and run down her pallid cheeks.

"Tears," he asked, "for me?"

He pulled her stiff, unyielding body into his arms. "No need to cry, Angel girl. I'll take you home."

He took her hand, led her outside, and vanished into the night, taking her with him.

****

Garmin prodded Angel along, half dragging her at times. As the lights of the city blinked faintly in the distance, he noticed she was tiring more quickly than he had anticipated. Her persistent wailing was starting to grate on his nerves. He was tempted to tie her hands and feet, stuff a sock in her mouth, and sling her across his shoulder like a sack of potatoes. But he was reluctant to return to the underworld with a bride looking like something that had been ravaged by a pack of hounds.

He stopped, put his fingers to his lips and whistled. The shrill sound was picked up and carried upward and outward by the force of windy gales that sprang up from nowhere.

A mighty steed appeared out of the night. His sleek, black coat blended perfectly with the shadows, making it hard to tell where the night ended and the horse began.

He picked up the woman and set her astride the beast. The horse jerked back, tossing his head and rolling his eyes. Garmin tugged sharply on the reins.

"Stand still, brute."

He leaped astride the stallion and wrapped his arms around the woman's waist. He patted the horse's neck and whispered in his ear.

"Go quickly and ever so quietly, Midnight. The Maiden can hear the grass grow."

The grand stallion galloped through the night as silent as a tomb. There was no audible sound of hooves striking against pavement. The only indication of their presence was the steamy breath from Midnight's nostrils shrouding the landscape in a dense, humid mist, and the occasional labored sigh from the woman.

He noticed as Angel lay against his chest, the closer they got to the bridge, the slower her heartbeat became and the more she labored for breath. He could find no reason for the downward spiral. Garmin Maximilian hadn't traveled such a great distance and invested his valuable time to have the woman expire within a few miles of journey's end.

He shook her none too gently. She was probably playing possum. If he found that was the case, he would drag the bitch the remainder of the way on her surly ass.

CHAPTER THIRTEEN

Garmin chastised himself for breaking his number one rule to never assume anything. He'd erred in thinking Angel would blindly follow him to the ends of the earth and beyond. This error in judgment had cost him dearly.

He had taken physical possession of Angel, but ultimately, she wasn't his. She had long since ceased struggling, but her eyes said betrayal and loathing more distinctly than any words could have done. Nothing was penetrating the cortexes of her brain, with the exception of thoughts of her damnable son.

Children! He could see no reason for them. Babies were disgusting little creatures that ate, regurgitated their food, defecated, screwed up their face and made an abominable noise hurtful to the ears. The incessant howling sent bitches running like idiots, wasting valuable time and affection on the little brats that was rightfully deserving of the master.

Angel, it seemed, was a natural in the art of mothering. In hindsight, perhaps he should have insisted on bringing Alex along on the journey instead of listening to his mother and leaving him behind. The little asswipe had the makings of a great warrior. He chuckled. The shapeshifting had been pure genius. The woman never suspected a thing, but Alex had been onto him from the beginning. Even his cloak of invisibility didn't work on the boy. He sighed deeply. No use crying over a deed done.

Whether Angel shared his feelings of love and passion, at this moment, was of little consequence. She would submit to his wants and desires, and he in return would clothe her lovely body in the finest gowns and choice of jewels. Her slightest wish would be his command, except for matters regarding the boy. The topic would be forever closed to discussion within the realms of his world…their world.

If she wanted children, he'd give her what she wanted, dozens of children. But he certainly would not wipe their snotty little noses or the even viler bottom end. He'd settle for the pleasure of creating little Kanimorphs and let her have the pleasure of tending the little demons.

The girls would look like her, of course. If he was lucky, the first child would be a boy, a special edition, featuring ancestral Kanimorph genes.

Garmin focused his thoughts on the hurdles at journey's end. He could ill afford idle wondering. Since he was carrying a hostile companion, his chances of crossing the bridge and reentering the realms of hell without a clash of wills with The Maiden were very slim to none. The old crone would've had ample time to figure out his escape had been by means of foul play. Under the right circumstances, all *may* have been forgiven, except for the tantalizing Judas kiss as he'd passed her by.

He allowed himself a satirical smile as he envisioned The Maiden's rage when she discovered he'd gotten past her sight unseen. Perhaps he'd tell her to get glasses. His smile widened. He doubted if those sentiments would cajole her into allowing him to cross the bridge again without a fight.

****

111

The road began to grow more familiar. Garmin could tell the bridge was nigh by the stench of the river and the clanking sounds of bones washing over one another, which were becoming a thunderous roar.

Soon, the keeper of the bridge would be able to detect their presence. She would be lying in wait. He could see her in his mind's eye, standing there night after night waiting and listening, chanting ancient spells of divination and enchanting the bridge to alert her if it was touched by as much as a single grain of sand. He would venture to guess the air would be charged with lightning bolts ready to strike with the precision of the finest archer.

With no way around The Maiden, he'd have to go through her, and time was not on his side. He figured his best approach would be a frontal attack. If he could get The Maiden worked up enough, she might forget about her bag of tricks and come after him one on one.

He felt Angel stir restlessly. He searched her face and felt fear nudge his heart. She was pale as death and leaned heavily against him, drifting in and out of consciousness with each step of his fine steed. His primal instinct warned him her condition was grave and, without help, death was imminent. What kind of help did she need? Why was she growing weaker? He was very efficient at killing, but a novice in the art of healing. For the first time, he felt helpless and afraid.

He stared down into the face resting against his shoulder and realized the mighty Garmin Maximilian had been taken down with a single blow to the heart. He'd come to love the girl he'd chosen for his mate. His wish to take a mate for the purpose of repopulating the Kanimorph species had become a burning desire for a life-time companion to reciprocate his love. He wanted a mate who would be honored to bear the fruit of his loins, as he'd be honored to call her wife. And he'd found her. An indulgent smile crossed his face. Angel just didn't know it yet. In time, she would learn to love and trust him again. She was a prize worthy of the wait. He would move heaven and earth and split hell wide open before he'd lose her.

The Maiden would know what to do. The sagacious, ancient old relic knew everything. He'd swallow his pride and ask her advice, beg if he had to. If he apologized profusely and explained his situation, maybe The Maiden would find it in her black heart to set aside her personal grievances and extend a helping hand toward the woman.

He laughed at his own foolishness. The Maiden had no heart. She was mean clean through to the bone.

Perhaps his best course of action would be to be-seech The Dark Mother's help. He'd pledge his undying allegiance for a thousand years, ten thousand years, for-ever, if she would use her mystical powers to heal his Angel. Time was not the enemy of two souls destined for eternity.

"Fool!"

The second idea was even more foolish than the first. The Dark Mother would most likely stay angry with him for decades, as she'd been known to do in the past.

He must hurry. The woman grew weaker with every passing moment he tarried on the wrong side of the bridge. He'd get across the bridge somehow. Once inside the great hall, he'd seek out The Dark Mother's forbid-

113

den grimoire and find his own cure.

He rode on for another mile. The faint gurgling sounds were not lost on his keen ears and the rise and fall of Angel's bosom was short and far between. He spoke to the horse.

"Stop, Midnight! The woman can go no farther."

He dismounted and laid Angel on a bed of soft moss beneath a clump of yew trees lining the edge of the over-grown path. A shooting star streaked across the sky. A good omen! He dared to hope.

He rubbed the horse's nose. "Stay with her, Midnight."

The horse shook his head up and down. Satisfied, Garmin disappeared into the blackness.

He paused at the edge of the clearing, hunkered down in the tall grass, and watched The Maiden pace back and forth with her neck extended and her nose pointed in his direction. He was not surprised to see she had already sensed his presence, and he could tell from the downward curl of her lips, she'd been looking forward to this moment with great anticipation.

"So, you've finally returned, you wretched thing!"

He stepped boldly into view, keeping both hands in plain sight. For the sake of Angel, he would humble himself and try the power of persuasion.

"Wait! I haven't returned alone and my companion is in dire need of medical attention. I need your help."

His plea was lost on The Maiden.

"You might have gotten out, but to get back in, you'll have to get by me! You may have fooled me once but—"

He took a step forward, his hand hovering near the hilt of his sword.

"Move aside, bitch. Don't make me kill you."

To his surprise, The Maiden obligingly moved a step sideways, but as he stepped forward, she swung savagely, connecting first with a right hook and then with a left. Bare knuckles cut into his flesh. Caught off guard, Garmin fell, sprawling backward. He leaped up and touched his tongue to his split lip. The unmistakable smell of blood stung his nostrils and quickened his pulse.

"You double-crossing she-devil! I'll filet your bony ass and feed you to the serpents."

He saw a sly grin spread The Maiden's leathery cheeks.

"The Dark Mother would not be pleased to lose her keeper of the bridge."

"The Dark Mother won't have any use for you after I get through wiping your pussy with my sword. When I'm done with you, there won't be enough left of your rotten hide for the maggots and dung beetles."

A raspy laugh wheezed in The Maiden's throat like death rattles. "Don't try to sweet talk me, honey."

He hit her with a roundhouse kick to the head. He watched slack-jawed as she rolled her eyes back in her head. The pupils disappeared from view. The whites of her eyes, infiltrated with red spider veins, stared out from the depths of sunken eye sockets setting every nerve ending in his body vibrating. He ground his teeth together and felt the urge to turn and flee, not from fear, but from the wretchedness of the wretched.

He moved in and delivered a quick chop to the throat. The impact tore through the mummified flesh and dislodged a couple of vertebrae in The Maiden's neck, tilting her head at a most peculiar angle. The bones skidded across the bridge and hung precariously off the edge as the water greedily lapped closer to the prize.

He waited as The Maiden danced after the skeletal debris, her feet barely scraping the surface of the bridge. He had to give her credit. The old thing was light footed. He found her efforts to hold her head erect, while stooping to snatch back the bones and watch him at the same time, extremely amusing.

It appeared this battle was over and done before it had gotten into full swing.

The laughter dried on his lips. Tiny pimples pushed the hairs on his arms and the back of his neck upward until they stood stiff and erect. His eyes bugged as The Maiden fitted the discs back into their hollow sockets and twisted her head a full 360-degree rotation.

"Damn!"

She had opened her bag of tricks. There would be no compromise and no turning back.

Garmin and The Maiden circled warily. He watched her eyes as she took the initiative and aggressively advanced forward. He saw her eyes shift downward a brief second before he felt his heels leave the surface of the bridge. He tottered on the edge, balancing on the balls of his feet. He glanced down at the breaking waves slapping against the bridge; then back at The Maiden moving in on him. There was nowhere to go but down!

A half-smile pushed up the corners of his lips. He bowed at the waist, then folded his arms across his chest and fell backward into the churning vortex, disappearing from sight underneath the bridge.

Garmin could feel the power surging through his coils as he shapeshifted. A giant anaconda rose out of the water. He was big and strong! He snatched The Maiden from behind as she stood peering into the river, gloating over her victory. He wrapped himself around her, rendering her helpless, and squeezed slowly, savoring the moment.

One minute, he was squeezing the life out of the wretched old river rat, and the next minute, she'd managed to rip loose one of her own rib bones and render him a painful jab.

Garmin hissed angrily and dropped her with a thump. The decrepit old sea hag needed to be taught a lesson before this battle was officially declared won. He changed back into his original form. In spite of his personal feelings, if The Maiden opted to save face by agreeing to allow safe passage across the bridge for Angel and him, he would postpone the inevitable.

Sooner or later, the two of them were going to lock horns and The Dark Mother would be looking for a replacement keeper of the bridge. Maybe today. It appeared The Maiden was still fuzzed and ready to fight!

He felt an annoying jolt as she came from behind and landed a glancing blow to his kidney that spun him around, and then excruciating pain as she followed up with a foot to the groin. Her hallux gouged into his scrotum with such force, he feared she'd impaled his nuts. Waves of nausea doubled him over. How dare she strike below the belt! Those sacks contained the last seed of the Kanimorph species.

He could hear screeching noises erupting from deep within The Maiden's diaphragm. She was holding her sides as spasms racked her body. It seemed as though her rib cage was on the verge of separating from the rest of her skeletal frame. Then it hit him. The bitch was laughing at him!

He shapeshifted into a large black panther. He took careful aim and hit her square in the face with a putrid urine cocktail. He changed back into his normal self, howling boisterously as she wiped her eyes and wrung cat urine from her tattered rags.

He thought of the woman he'd left in the woods. She could be dying with only Midnight to comfort her while he engaged in a pissing contest with this cold, heartless sea donkey. He was through playing. Negotiations had broken down. He would have to forcefully take the bridge and throw himself on the mercy of The Dark Mother.

He changed to his Kanimorph form. His saber teeth glowed white against his bronze skin and his claws came out long, sharp, curved like scimitars. He struck at her.

The Maiden fell to the bridge and curled into a ball trying to shield her vital organs. He could smell her fear like a palpable force. He pounced on her, ripping away rotting flesh from her body as his monstrous jaws snapped shut around her bony neck. He lifted her and shook her like a rag doll.

She managed to squeak out, "Truce! A life for a life."

"What did you say?" he asked.

"I know about your secret in the woods," she whispered hoarsely.

He held her high. "What do you know, you wretched old bag of bones?"

"Death is searching the woods for the one you call Angel," she chanted, the words gurgling in her throat.

Garmin's voice whistled through the neck bones

clamped tightly between his teeth.

"What do you know of my Angel?"

He permitted her feet to touch the bridge and lightened the pressure of his jaws a little, allowing her to speak more clearly. The flicker of anxiety in his eyes was not lost on The Maiden. She smirked knowingly.

"Turn me loose and promise to do me no harm and I'll offer a trade!"

He loosened his hold. "You're in no position to bargain, witch. One second is how long it'll take to sever your head from the rest of your miserable frame."

He was tempted to chomp down and decapitate the pretentious old hag, but her words struck a chord of fear into his heart. He suddenly realized he was shaking The Maiden so violently that her bones were rattling. He threw her down on the bridge and waited, tensed and ready. He could sense the struggle raging inside her, but her eyes remained low, signaling defeat, and her body went limp in surrender.

He spoke through clenched teeth. "You cross me and I'll not only take your head, I'll carry the horrible thing to the other side of the bridge and bury it deep. You've always managed to hocus-pocus your parts back together, but not this time!"

"Truce!" she repeated. "Truce!"

"Now, what do you know of my secret in the woods?" He advanced a step forward. "If you have harmed—"

"No! No! I swear I've not touched her."

The Maiden remained cowered low in submission, but her face twisted into a half-smile. "I see more than you know," she mumbled.

119

Garmin took another step forward. "Death? You said Death was stalking the woods. What is his purpose?"

He lifted her chin and stared at her face, but she refused to meet his gaze.

"He won't find her. If you hurry, I'm willing to let you cross the bridge freely, the girl, too, if you're prepared to suffer the consequences of your actions. But before I say anything more, I want your vow you'll spare me. Swear it on the life of the woman!"

He reflected for a moment. "What's to stop me from finishing you off and carrying Angel across to safety on my terms?"

He saw a flicker of malice in The Maiden's eyes. She laughed, a spiteful, calculated sound originating from her gut, then trickling off to a gurgle at the base of her throat.

"You don't know the whole secret."

He wanted to bitch slap the sly grin off that psychoslut's face, but he had to know what she was holding back.

"You can destroy me easy enough," she said, "but if you do, you've sealed your own fate!"

Suspicion glinted in his eyes, but he sensed her words were more than a ploy to save her own skin. She had him by the balls. He was weary of this façade. A dark scowl shadowed his face. He spoke. His voice, scarcely above a whisper, impacted like a clap of thunder.

"If you have something to say, spit it out!"

"One of my gifts is scrying," said The Maiden. "I see what I see, but Death and I have not conspired to take your woman away from you. Immortality is not gifted.

The price we mortals pay is steep, a curse if you will."

He growled angrily and extended his claws full length. "If you have cursed my beloved, you'll pray death takes you instead of her. Remove the curse, you revolting old horse turd!" He began to count. "One…two." He raised his hand. "Three—"

"I can't," she whispered. "It is a part of the parcel of the dark kingdom. This is the land of the dead, you imbecile! You, of all people, should know mortals cannot live here. If you bring the woman across this bridge, she will cease to exist in her world, and within a short while, this one as well." A strange expression crossed her face. "If she's lucky," she added.

His hands circled The Maiden's neck. "Liar!" Garmin shouted.

"Wait!" she cried. "I have kept my word. Did I not warn you there would be consequences?"

He looked toward the iron gates at the other end of the bridge. Armored with heavy metal chains and enormous padlocks, the gates were an impregnable force. Chances of breaching the security of the hallowed halls were slim. He threw back his head and screamed curses at the sky. His anguished cries skipped across the river reducing its raging fury to icy dunes.

He half expected The Dark Mother to step outside her door to see what the commotion was about. He hoped she did. If what The Maiden said was true, The Dark Mother was his last hope. He'd plead with her to lift the curse, bend the rules, whatever it took to save Angel's life.

If The Dark Mother refused, he'd fight her to the death, eat her heart and gain all her knowledge. Then, he could figure it out for himself. Angel and he, sitting side by side on matching thrones would be awesome.

What was he thinking? The Dark Mother was invincible. His rogue thoughts were enough to set his rapport with her back five hundred years. She had an army of boot licking toads at her disposal who would like nothing better than claim his coveted position. But that was not her way. She had built him from the ground up and would dismantle him quicker than a heartbeat once she was done with him. She liked to dish out her own brand of justice, and she held the secret ingredients in the recipe for pain.

He chuckled dryly. She was not called The Dark Mother without cause. Some mistakenly believed she wore the black hooded robe to shield one side of her face because legend claimed that to look upon her beauty full face would stop the heart of any man. But he knew the truth. Once, he'd accidentally entered the room while she was disrobing, and the dark side hidden beneath her cowl chilled the marrow in his bones. However, her title did not reflect her abominable disfiguration, but her soul…black as sin and as unyielding as the ironwood forest.

The Dark Mother and he tolerated each other well. She pampered him with the finest cuisine, a soft, warm bed, stylish attire, and free reign to a stable of high-spirited bitches to mount whenever he felt an urge to ride.

Her only requisite was to wear the symbolic collar and chain, and he did so reluctantly as a gesture of his sworn dedication and obedience. He followed The Dark Mother's orders without question. When she needed a job done, he did it without hesitation or conscious thought, and did the job right.

He glanced at The Maiden and caught her watching him. She appeared a little apprehensive as if she was holding a secret. He locked her gaze with his and held it.

"What are you not telling me? There must be a way. Speak!"

Her gaze darted aside, but he cupped her chin and held her face steady.

Her words were an arrow to his heart.

"The woman is too close to the gate. The fine line between this world and her world has been breached. Soon the shadow of death will find her. She will die, whether or not she crosses the bridge, and if you don't get back on this side soon, you'll join her. I've sensed your immortality draining away, seeping into the ground and drawing your soul after it. You are strong, but tarry much longer and the mighty Garmin will lose the ultimate battle!"

He listened in stunned silence. He could sense she still harbored thoughts of breaking down his defenses, hoping she could take him out and restore her pride and mend her bruised ego, but he sensed something else even more sinister and deadly. She was telling the truth!

"Silence!" he roared. "If what you say is true, it matters not if I should die as long as Angel may live. I've got to get her away from this place."

"Fool!" she muttered. "Fool! Do what you must."

He raced back along the path he came as if his life depended on it, and indeed it seemed it did, both his and the woman's.

He longed to call to Midnight, his loyal companion,

but if he was to be successful in his mission, stealth was of the utmost importance.

Even Death must have a weakness, a crack of some sort in his armor, and by the gods, he was going to find it. He'd fight with every ounce of strength left in his body until the last breath to keep this manifestation of wickedness from stripping him of the one thing he'd ever held dear. Although he realized deep down in his core, in a firefight outside the realm of The Dark Mother's jurisdiction, Death would walk away victorious.

He glimpsed a shadow and sped after it. If he was quick, he could whisk Angel beyond the dominion of the Dark Lord's authority until the date predestined by the hands of fate for *her* mortal time and place.

Throwing caution to the wind, he rushed forward, crashing through the underbrush. Thorns tore his flesh, but he was beyond feeling. The risks to his own mortality paled against the fate that awaited his true love. Once Angel was safe, he would attend to the trivial details of his own destiny.

CHAPTER FOURTEEN

The yew trees under which Angel lay stirred gently as if caressed by a soft breeze, but the air was still, thick, and unsustainable. She drifted in and out of consciousness, gaping like a fish out of water. She tried to rationalize the series of events that had brought her to this strange place, but nothing made sense.

She recalled vividly the ride in the limousine, the wine and the sweet taste of a man's kiss on her lips. Only, the man she knew as Garmin wasn't a man. He was a beast with balls the size of goose eggs and a penis that dragged halfway down his knees.

She squeezed her eyelids and tried to blot the image of the creature from her mind. Her brain refused to process the overall picture in its entirety, just bits and pieces at a time. It appeared as if nature had taken a man and a beast, scrambled their atoms, and reassembled them into a mutant species that walked and talked like a man, bore the physical characteristics of a beast, but could claim kinship with neither.

Images of the man, beast, and a humongous black dog flashed before her eyes, each image surrealistically superimposing over the other until only the beast was left. The implication of those images could only mean that the man, beast, and dog were one and the same.

"Sweet Jesus!"

Waves of blackness washed over her and she didn't have to think about it anymore.

She was nuzzled awake by the magnificent black stallion. He snorted, blowing great whiffs of his misty breath on her face, which surprisingly seemed to ease the pressure on her tortured lungs. She grasped the low hanging tree branches and tried to pull herself to her feet. When the beastly *thing* returned, she wanted to be far away from this God-forsaken place.

She fell back weakly as the stark truth of her situation hit home. She was completely at the mercy of her captor and didn't even know what kind of monster had claimed her as his bride. She tried to focus on the man who first identified himself with the name Madd, and later changed it to Garmin, but the image of the beast pushed everything aside.

His eyes haunted her. Whatever else he might be, the eyes were human. He had dropped his guard for an instant and, reflected within the deep-set golden pools of amber, she had glimpsed Garmin's very soul. What she saw left no doubt the feelings he professed to have for her were real. She was comforted to know she wasn't in any immediate danger of being harmed by the creature, but sex with that animal was out of the question. It was humanly impossible. A hollow sound passed through her lips, a dry brittle sigh of hopelessness. The beast fully intended to consummate the demonship he referred to as coupling. Her lips moved in a silent prayer for salvation.

She thought of Alex and began to cry. She regretted her hasty words, which had forced Garmin to leave her son behind. In an attempt to spare her baby whatever fate awaited her, she'd placed him at an even greater risk. What would happen to him now that she was gone?

The Man had made promises of immortality and life everlasting, but she'd been growing steadily weaker day after day since she'd been shanghaied and forced to travel on this insidious road to hell. There was no explanation for her strange affliction, but something was drawing her strength, sucking the life from her body.

She'd seen the concern registered on Garmin's face and heard it in his voice. He knew it, too! He'd vowed to come back for her, but unless he returned soon, it might be too late.

Perhaps he wouldn't come back at all. She'd certainly not given him a reason to do so. The trip had not been a pleasant one for him. She'd fought against it every step of the way. Now, at journey's end, she had a chance to mount this noble stallion, Midnight, and ride back the way she'd come, but she simply could not force herself to go and leave Garmin behind. God help her! Was she such a pathetically sad case that she had feelings for a beast? In her heart, she knew it was true.

Somewhere beneath his grisly exterior beat the heart of the man she had come to love with every fiber of her being. Her body ached for his touch; the man, not the hideous monster that had stood before her offering his heart and claw, professing an unthinkable union and making promises beyond her wildest imaginations.

His ace in the hole had been immortality, a nice fantasy, but even more unbelievable than the fountain of youth. She laughed hysterically. He had also promised untold wealth: rubies, diamonds, emeralds, and gold nuggets the size of field rocks. Men were such liars!

With death treading on her heels, it really didn't matter. She'd trade it all for a chance to hold Garmin in her arms and tell him how much she loved him, and a chance to say goodbye to her baby boy.

In the distance, low hanging black clouds churned in the morning sky. The approaching wave of blackness seemed to coincide with the numbing cold penetrating her body, stiffening her limbs and slowing her heart rate to a mere flutter. She could sense a shadowy presence creeping nearer with each passing moment and instinctively knew it was coming for her. She shivered and stared in the direction Garmin had gone. She had to think of him as a man. The stress of dealing with the truth was too overwhelming.

She gathered all her strength and drew the remnants of her courage around her like a warm blanket. Even though the end seemed inevitable, she clung to hope, refusing to give up the ghost.

"Not yet," she whispered timidly, then more defiantly, "Not yet!"

She waited with the temerity of an Amazon warrior. Garmin would protect her from this evil. He'd come for her. She knew this with a certainty that comes from the heart. He'd come and she'd go with him. Love would find a way to bless this hellish union.

She'd go willingly, but not unconditionally. Alex and she came as a pair. He must take both or neither. She'd gladly render up her life for Garmin's, but she wouldn't compromise the life of her child. If he could accept the extra baggage she brought to this union and love her son as he did her, she could forgive his deceitfulness in winning her heart.

She'd be whatever he wanted her to be. In time, she could come to accept this form so alien to anything she'd ever seen that her mind had all but blocked out the details.

His outward appearance was only a shell. What was inside mattered in the overall scheme of things. She wanted to tell Garmin this. She must tell him! But she was so tired. She'd rest a bit, close her eyes for a moment, and then she'd go in search of her love, crawling on her hands and knees if necessary.

She had to convince him to go back for Alex. She didn't care anymore about the world she called home, just as long as the three of them were together.

CHAPTER FIFTEEN

As the sprawling branches of the ancient yew trees came into view, Garmin's eyes scanned the terrain for signs of danger. The movement of the grass warned him his unconquerable foe was closing fast. He rounded the bend and saw Angel. She sat leaned against a tree, her chest rising and falling so slowly, he feared she was not breathing at all.

Midnight stood beside her, his head lowered and his muzzle pressed against her face as if contact with another living creature could prevent life from escaping her frail body.

He rushed forward and fell on his knees beside her. He rubbed her icy hands and mopped beads of perspiration from her brow with the tail of his shirt. The clamminess of her skin chilled him to the marrow. He gathered her in his arms and kissed her pale cheeks, begging her to speak to him.

He trembled with desire, not a burning in the loins, but a passion of the heart, a yearning to be her lover, her friend, her protector, anything she wanted him to be, even human, if it pleased her.

He felt her stir in his arms. He caught his breath, not daring to move as she wrapped both arms around his neck.

"I knew you'd return for me," she whispered. "Now that you've come, not even death can keep us apart. If we must die, we'll die together, my love, but if the promise of immortality is for real, we'll be together forever."

He looked longingly into the depths of her soul

through eyes staring at him trustingly. He sighed heavily. It was not meant to be, not here, not now. Some-day…someday love would build its own bridge. He kissed Angel tenderly and lifted her to her feet. He re-moved the gold chain from his neck and slipped it over her head.

"My heart to your heart," he whispered. "As long as the links are unbroken, our hearts shall beat as one, bound together for all time."

He lifted her and set her astride Midnight. "We must ride," he said and turned his face away so she couldn't read the lie in his eyes. "Our son, Alex, will be waiting."

Splinters from his broken heart impaled his soul as Angel smiled at him and extended her hand to boost him up behind her. He reached out and touched her finger-tips, then raised his hand and slapped Midnight on the flank.

"Go!" he shouted. "Run like the wind. Take the woman back to her world and return swiftly."

His heart felt as if it was being wrenched from his chest as she screamed out his name. The sound trailed off into an eerie wail as Midnight jetted out of sight.

Straightening his shoulders, he headed back toward the bridge. His footsteps faltered and his strength waned. He was weak and vulnerable, but he did not despair. He was Garmin Maximilian. In his chest beat the heart of a great warrior. If he was destined to die today, he would do so with dignity and without fear. He had spirited An-gel away from Death's bony fingers, and if his life was demanded in payment, Death could have it. He laughed. Death could claim no victory when one willingly sacri-ficed his life for another.

He walked slowly. There was no reason to hurry now. Death was closing in behind him and The Maiden was lurking on the bridge ahead. His fate was sealed. The question remaining was what to do about his precarious situation. He wouldn't go peacefully, of course, that wasn't his nature. He stumbled and righted himself, willing his limbs to keep moving. The Maiden mustn't know the extent of his weakened condition, or she'd finish him off before he could strike a single blow. He wanted to take the vibrations of steel striking bone to whatever fate awaited.

Out of the corner of his eye, he glimpsed a dark shadow at his back. He pivoted around and lashed out with his last ounce of strength. He was rewarded by the sound of a quick intake of breath and a stifled grunt of surprise. He felt the ground tremble.

He sensed he was no longer being pursued, but he wasn't conceited enough to think he'd finished off his adversary; he had merely stalled him for a few moments.

The bridge loomed ahead. If he could make it across, he'd be on hallowed ground, a sanctuary for immortals.

He plodded on by willpower alone: twenty feet, fifteen, seven, putting one foot in front of the other. His knees buckled. He fell, grinding his face into a pillar at the base of the bridge. He stretched out his arms and felt the roughly hewn boards beneath his hands. The dirt clogging his nostrils told him most of his body was still on fertile ground, which boded ill for his kind. His energy was being sponged from him, and he could sense his adversary was on the move again, and closing in fast.

He clawed at the bridge. Splinters pierced his fingers and jabbed deep underneath his nails as he struggled to drag his useless limbs onto the bridge. He was too weak. He cursed the avenger that pursued him so relentlessly, the earth for sapping the energy from his body, The Maiden on the bridge, and The Dark Mother, until the words would no longer pass through his lips.

He raised his head and waited for the end to come. He would not bow before death. Garmin Maximilian would go out proudly with his chin held high. He faded in and out of consciousness, his vision becoming blurred and his thoughts incoherent.

"Grab onto my hand," a crackly voice said close to his ear.

He opened his eyes and focused his attention on the direction of the voice. The Maiden stood in front of him, her feet planted firmly on the bridge, her bony hand outstretched, and a strange glint in her eye.

"Take it!" she urged him. "I must tell you—"

He could feel himself slipping away and he was glad. He didn't care to hear what the old bag had to say, and he certainly didn't want the image of her face to follow him into the snake pit.

Through the deepest realm of his subconscious, he could hear the clash of swords and feel his body being dragged across the bridge, one inch at a time.

He awakened inside the iron gates of The Dark Mother's palace with no idea of how he came to be there. He could see a dark shadowy form at the far end of the bridge howling in rage and shaking a broken sword at The Maiden.

He was startled to see she paid no mind to the shadow, but watched him from the bridge's edge, being careful not to step outside her bounds and invade his space. He sprang to his feet as she drew herself up to her full five foot frame.

"I lied," she said, nervously knotting her fingers together. "Mortals can cross, but the victory is short lived and the price is too high. Sooner or later the soul will be sucked from any mortal being who dares to tempt fate, leaving only an empty vessel." She stabbed at her bony chest with her finger and cackled loudly, a haunting sound full of sadness, grief, despair, jealousy, loneliness, and uncensored raw hatred. Strangely, Garmin didn't feel The Maiden's animosity was directed at him.

His fingers gripped the hilt of his sword as she reached underneath the bridge and retrieved a sword like none he had ever seen. If it had been anyone other than The Maiden, he would have sworn her eyes misted as she extended her arm with the weapon pointed downward.

"Take it," she said in a trembling voice. "It can defy Death and penetrate the shroud of immortality."

He eyed her suspiciously. It was indeed a fine piece of weaponry. He stepped outside the iron bars and took it. It was perfectly balanced and felt good in his hand as if it had been forged especially for him. The old woman was up to something. He just didn't know what.

He drew his own sword. He ignored The Maiden's outstretched hand and with a flick of his wrist, cast his blade into the river. He stared at her hard, sheathed the gifted sword, and disappeared into the great hall, clanging the huge wooden door shut behind him.

He sought out The Dark Mother. He wanted to tell her about Angel. Implore her to help him find a way to bring his heart's desire *home*.

He found her sitting on her golden throne. One

hand gripped a crystal skull hand rest, and the other, hidden beneath the sleeve of her black robe, dangled down and stroked the first head of the beast sitting at her side.

He paused in the doorway, and for the first time *really* looked at her. His eyes darkened. Was he destined to be alone for all eternity like The Dark Mother?

For a fleeting second, something akin to joy flitted across The Dark Mother's face, then her eyes iced over and her mouth puckered in malice.

"So you decided to come back to me, did you? I wondered if you would."

"I gave my word," Garmin said. "As did you."

She sat perfectly still, staring at him. "You know very well it was never my intention to allow you to go. I only agreed to such a bizarre arrangement because I didn't think you'd be able to get past the incompetent moron guarding the bridge."

"But you did agree."

He shifted his feet and looked sheepish.

"Truth be told, I owe the keeper of the bridge a debt of gratitude. She pulled me from the clutches of Death and put me safely inside the iron gates. In all fairness, The Maiden never had a clue until it was too late." He chuckled. "One can't defend against what one can't see." He spread his arms. "Now you see me." He vanished into thin air. "Now you don't," he said, then popped back into view. "The Maiden *did* sound the alarm, but nobody listened."

The knuckles showed white on The Dark Mother's hand, and her fingers lay still on the head of the beast.

"Most would be afraid to admit such treachery. I

shall take that into consideration when deciding your punishment."

Garmin pulled back his shoulders and lifted his chin. He was afraid of nothing! He was a warrior. Fear was not a word in his vocabulary. He cowered before no one, not even Big Bad Mama.

He had known, deep down inside, The Dark Mother would renege on their agreement. After all, she'd had twenty-seven days to stew about it. A little longer would not have added any more flavor to the pot. He should've stayed with Angel a while longer, given her time to digest the idea of a new world and new life before whisking her away like a thief in the night.

He was glad he'd sent her back...to her son. At least, she'd be happy, and that was all that mattered for the moment. Someday...

He didn't so much as bat an eye when The Dark Mother motioned him forward. He took a step and stood before her, his face devoid of expression and his head held high. His hand eased toward the sword at his side as the beast bared its teeth and strained against the short leash shackling it to the leg of The Dark Mother's throne.

"Kneel," she commanded.

He dropped to one knee, but his gaze never faltered from The Dark Mother's face. She leaned forward and whispered in his ear, then sat back and studied his face, but found only a blank canvas.

He stood and gave a slight nod. "As you wish, Dark Mother."

He turned on his heel and strode from the room.

Lucid Dreams

****

Garmin selected the largest, juiciest steak in his larder, cooked it to perfection, and placed it on a silver platter. He piled on a dozen yeast rolls, dripping with freshly churned butter, and poured a mug of ale. He stepped outside the iron gates and placed the platter on the bridge, then stepped back and hunkered down, watching The Maiden warily as she approached the offering.

She seemed not to notice him as she ravenously devoured the meat, savoring every morsel. She finished off the sweet rolls, licking the butter from her fingers, then turned up the mug of ale and downed it without taking the cup from her lips. Garmin winced as she rubbed her belly and belched loudly.

He stood and stepped onto the bridge. The Maiden neither retreated nor showed any sign of animosity. She laughed. The soft tinkling tones were totally out of character. It triggered a memory from a time and place Garmin thought were merely figments of his imagination. He stood motionless as she picked up the empty silver tray and extended it toward him. An unspoken *'thank you'* quivered on her lips.

Garmin took a step forward, drew his sword and ran her through.

The silver tray fell from her hand and clattered onto the bridge. She reached out and clutched his sleeve.

"My son," she whispered and crumpled in a heap at his feet.

Garmin didn't blink. He wiped his blade on the leg of his trousers and aimed a highly polished boot at the heap of bones, but The Maiden's remains had already disintegrated into dust.

Sheathing his sword, he walked back through the iron gates. He paused a moment to watch a dirt devil spawn from the bone ashes, twist its way across the bridge, and dissipate beyond the gateway to eternity, spreading The Maiden's ashes on fertile soil, setting her spirit free.

He wiped his eyes. "Rest in peace, Mama," he said and disappeared inside the castle where The Dark Mother waited.

At that precise moment, time ceased to matter to the immortal Garmin Maximilian; but eternity cannot be measured by the tick of a clock or the rise and set of the sun; neither does time take precedence over matters of the heart. His eyes glinted with determination. Angel could not come to him, but he could go to her. One month, six months, a year, for all eternity, his feelings for her would not change, but he would not wait long. If he was unable to find a loophole before one earth year had passed, he'd make one. His fingers polished the hilt of his sword, and he smiled.

CHAPTER SIXTEEN

In the bowels of New York City, days turned to weeks and weeks to months. At first glance, it seemed nothing had changed. The streetwalkers still stood on their favorite corners, drug dealers peddled their poisons, and crime ran rampant. But Angel McKeough had changed.

For the past nine months, she'd spent most of her time in her small shoebox second story apartment. Day in and day out, she sat draped in a heavy gold chain, fingering the links as if it was a rosary, reciting the fifteen promises.

The neon lights and billboard signs shined through the window, highlighting the fullness of her belly. There was no denying a baby was growing inside her, but she had no recollection of how it came to be there.

She sensed her time was drawing near. She was big enough to be carrying twins, but the doctor said, "No"! She couldn't shake the feeling something wasn't right. Alex had weighed a whopping eight pounds, but this baby was bigger, stronger and more demanding. Every time she thought about the baby, she was thrown into a state of panic.

The baby's kicks had changed from a flutter to solid contacts against the inside of her womb so forceful it felt as though he was sucker punching her in the abdomen. She wanted this baby; she loved him, but she was afraid. She was torn because she didn't know if she was afraid for the baby or if she was afraid of the baby.

Since her *accident*, her mind couldn't seem to differentiate between fantasy and reality, the result of some sort of brain trauma the doctors said, a head injury perhaps. Even the nature of the accident was a mystery. The doctors could offer no plausible explanation for the selected memory loss, leaving her with unanswered questions. The father must have been a real jackass. Perhaps her memory loss was a good thing.

Her memory was beginning to come back in bits and pieces that seemed more like a bad dream. She wondered if the truth would set her free or push her over the edge.

She idly counted the links on the gold chain hanging around her neck. The heavy chain was another unsolved mystery. The thing must be worth a fortune, but she couldn't bring herself to part with it. Where had it come from? Why did she feel such a connection with the damned thing? She had a gut feeling that somehow the chain held the answers she so desperately sought. She was weary of trying to figure it out. She just wanted the nightmare to end.

For nine long months, she'd struggled with her illness and tried to come to terms with her immaculate conception. Those bitches and sons-of-bitches at the club seemed to think she was faking amnesia to avoid revealing the identity of the child's father.

Rumors spread. The disinformation led to wagers and had fingers pointing in all directions. Who? When? Where? These three words were on everybody's lips as they eagerly awaited the birth of her child.

Once the baby came, she hoped his tiny little face would trigger an image of his father, shake something loose in her brain, anything to jog her memory. The low-life bastard had knocked her up and seemingly disappeared from the face of the earth.

"Heaven has no rage like love to hatred turned."
She intoned the words softly, almost reverently. Old William Congreve really had that one pegged right. She knew a thing or two about fury and hatred. She'd been let go from *Club Venus* when she started showing she carried, as if the sight of a pregnant girl at a gentlemen's club would shame the men and send them running home to girlfriends, wives and children.

She'd been knocked up by an invisible man, and almost lost her mind in the process. She laughed bitterly. Life didn't play fair. She'd been screwed…might as well get tattooed. She grabbed a notepad and sketched a butterfly, the symbol of freedom, then scribbled the word *Madd* in bold red letters across its wings. The word had a distinct ring to it, short and to the point.

She was mad, mad as hell, and she wanted the whole damn world to know why. She'd have the tattoo placed in a prominent spot. When people asked what the inscription meant, she'd say men were dogs; cowardly, silver-tongued jackals who deserved to have their balls whacked off and run through a meat grinder. She would be more than glad to explain what *Madd* was all about!

The idea that a woman needed a man was the egotistical posturing of male chauvinist pigs. Through the hard times, she had found out one thing. Angel McKeough was a survivor. Once the baby was born, she intended to move her children out of this cesspool district of the city and take her life back. She was perfectly capable of standing on her own two feet.

She moved to the window and stared down at the people jostling each other, in a hurry to get nowhere. Was the man who fathered her child out there somewhere? Had he also fallen victim to a set of circumstances that had stolen his memory? Was he searching for answers…searching for her?

She straightened her shoulders and rubbed her belly. She hoped he would find her. Her child needed his father.

A baby was supposed to be a new beginning. Her precious little angel was going to start life with two strikes against him. The mystery surrounding the conception had made her the brunt of cruel jokes. She pretended not to hear the snide remarks and snickers when she walked down the street. Her baby was not *somebody's* child. He was her child, her own flesh and blood. If the father was too chickenshit to step forward and own up to his responsibilities for her unborn child, she's raise him on her own the way she's been forced to do with Alex.

She pulled Alex onto her lap. He patted her tummy. "My brother."

Angel's brow wrinkled in concentration. She'd spent nine months trying to figure a way out of the mess she'd gotten herself into. Her pregnancy was not a mess, but a blessing. The first genuine smile in a very long time started in her eyes and spread to her lips.

"That's right, sweetheart, your baby brother."

She wrapped her arms around Alex, cradling both her children. Her boys and she would be just fine. Love would find a way to keep her family together. The man who fathered her unborn child would come to her. She believed that with all her heart, and faith could move mountains. Sometimes, she could sense him watching over her. It gave her hope. Strangely, that was enough.

Lucid Dreams

About the author

Josephene Stull has always loved to write. However, life took a number of twists and turns before she actually committed to pursuing her dream of becoming a published author. Her dream came true when her first novel, co-authored with Carolyn Owens, titled *Witches, Bitches, and Good Ol' Boys*, was published by Solstice Publishing in 2012.

She shares fifteen acres in the heart of the Blue Grass State with her hubby, five dogs, and a royal stub tail cat named Caesar. She enjoys spending time with a wonderful son, four grandsons, and a host of other family and friends. She loves taking long walks. It allows her to feel the sun on her face, sing as loudly and off key as she likes and communes with her fur and feathered friends in the wild.

To learn more about Josephene Stull visit her pages:

Twitter: https://twitter.com/JoStull
Facebook: https://www.facebook.com/josephene.stull
https://www.facebook.com/pages/Author-Josephene-O-Stull-One-Step-at-a-Time/192429510826748
Website: http://www.TheGreasedQuill.com

Books by Josephene Stull

Witches, Bitches, and Good old Boys
co-authored with Carolyn Owens

Appalachian pride, loyalty and horror, mixed with a little mischief, mayhem and moonshine, create a series of events best described as a little bit of naughtiness, a bit of foolishness, and a whole lot of fun *Southern Style*.

Small town USA and city life is different as catfish and caviar, but laughter is universal, making *Witches, Bitches and Good Ol' Boys* a good source of amusement for any-one, including readers abroad.

Solstice Publishing, 2012
http://www.amazon.com/dp/B0078YKJLQ